100—

TO MENSA,
HAPPY BIRTHDAY
AND
BEST WISHES
FOR ASCENSION
6.7.75
FROM
RUSS

Turtle Diary

Turtle Diary

RUSSELL HOBAN

JONATHAN CAPE
THIRTY BEDFORD SQUARE LONDON

FIRST PUBLISHED 1975
© RUSSELL HOBAN 1975

JONATHAN CAPE LTD,
30 BEDFORD SQUARE, LONDON WCI

ISBN 0 224 01085 9

*Extract on pp. 42–44 by courtesy of the Trustees of the
National Maritime Museum, Greenwich*

SET IN 12 on 13 POINT CASLON (128)

PRINTED AND BOUND IN GREAT BRITAIN
BY BUTLER & TANNER LTD
FROME AND LONDON

To Ben

I

William G.

I don't want to go to the Zoo any more.

The other night I dreamt of an octopus. He was dark green, almost black, dark tentacles undulating in brown water. Not sure what colour an octopus is really. Found colour photos in two of the books at the shop. One octopus was brown and white, the other was grey, pinky, brown. They change colour it seems. Their eyes are dreadful to look at. I shouldn't like to be looked at by an octopus no matter how small and harmless it might be. To be stared at by those eyes would be altogether too much for me, would leave me nothing whatever to be. There was a black-and-white photo of octopuses hung up to dry on a pole at Thasos on the Aegean Sea, black against the sky, black bags hanging, black tentacles drooping and drying, behind them the brightness over the sea. They're related to the chambered nautilus which I'd always thought of only as a shell with nothing in it. But there it was in the book full of tentacles and swimming inscrutably.

Then I wanted to see an octopus. On Friday, my half-day at the shop, I went to the Zoo. Grey day, raining a little. Went in by the North Gate past the owls. *Bubo* this and *Bubo* that, each one sitting on its bar with wet feathers and implacable eyes. Over the bridge past the Aviary towering high against the sky, a huge pointy steel-mesh thing of gables and angles full of strange cries and dark flappings. There were little shrill children eating things. There was steam coming up in the rain from three square plates in the paving at the end of the bridge. Two girls and a boy bathed their bare legs in it. The tunnel on the other side of the bridge was echoing with children. Copies of cave-paintings on the walls of the tunnel. They didn't belong there, looked heavy-handed, false. One wanted to see SPURS, ARSENAL.

Very dark in the Aquarium. Green windows, things swimming. People black against the windows murmuring, explaining to children, holding them up, putting them down, urging them on, calling them back. Echoing footsteps of children running in the dark. Very shabby in the Aquarium, very small. Too many little green windows in the dark. Crabs, lobsters, two thornback rays, a little poor civil-servant-looking leopard shark. Tropical fish, eels, toads, frogs and newts. There was no octopus.

Sea turtles. Two or three hundred pounds the big ones must have weighed. Looping and swinging, flying in golden-green silty water in a grotty little tank no bigger than my room. Soaring, dipping and curving with flippers like wings in a glass box of second-hand ocean. Their eyes said nothing, the thousands of miles of ocean couldn't be said.

I thought: when I was a child I used to like the Zoo. The rain had stopped. I went to the Reptile House. No. Didn't want to see the snakes on hot sand under bright lights behind glass. Left the Reptile House, approached the apes. The gorilla lay on his stomach in his cell, his chin resting on his folded arms. No. I couldn't think which was worse: if he could remember or if he couldn't.

8

I went out of the Zoo to the 74 bus stop at the North Gate. There was a young woman with a little boy and girl. Maybe the boy was eight or nine. He had a little black rubber gorilla on a bit of elastic tied to a string and he danced the little black gorilla up and down in a little puddle, spat spat spat, not splashing. It was only a bit of wet on the pavement.

'Stop that,' said his mother. 'I told you to stop that.'

2

Neaera H.

I fancied a china castle for the aquarium but they had none at the shop, so I contented myself with a smart plastic shipwreck. Snugg & Sharpe are expecting a new Gillian Vole story from me but I have not got another furry-animal picnic or birthday party in me. I am tired of meek and cuddly creatures, my next book will be about a predator. I've posted my cheque for 31p to Gerrard & Haig in Surrey for a Great Water-beetle, *Dysticus marginalis*, and I should have it by tomorrow. I've asked for a male.

On my way home wheeling the tank and all the other aquarium gear in the push-chair I stopped at the radio and TV shop because there was an oyster-catcher on all the TV screens in the window, a B.B.C. nature film it must have been. It was like encountering someone from childhood now famous. I used to see oyster-catchers sometimes on the mussel beds near Breydon Bridge when the tide was out. They were nothing like the gulls and terns, their black-and-white had a special air, they went a little beyond being birds. They walked with their heads down, looking as if they had hands clasped behind their backs like little European philosophers in yachting gear. But it was a less rhythmical walk than a philosopher's because the oyster-catchers were busy making a living with the mussels. In childhood at Breydon Water the day was wide and quiet, there was time enough to think of everything with no hurry whatever, to look at everything many times over.

The oyster-catcher on the TV screens was gone, there was a shot of mudflats and sea. The oyster-catcher had been very elegant in colour: creamy white, velvety black, orange bill and eye-rings, pink legs. On the black-and-white screens it had been more existential, a working bird alone in the world. Here I am, I thought, forty-three years old, waiting for a water-beetle. My married friends wear Laura Ashley dresses and in their houses are grainy photographs of them barefoot on continental beaches with their naked children. I live alone, wear odds and ends, I have resisted vegetarianism and I don't keep cats.

I passed the place where they're tearing up the street and the three workmen in the hole said 'Good morning' for the first time. Before this we've nodded.

As I was going into my flat Webster de Vere, the un-employed actor next door, was coming out of his. 'Fascinating hobby,' he said when he saw the tank. 'I've been keeping fish for years. Black Mollies, you know. Nothing flash, just neat little black fish. What will you have in your aquarium?'

'A water-beetle,' I said.

'A water-beetle,' he said. 'Fascinating pet. If you ever need any snails do let me know, I've masses of them. Keep the tank clean, you know.'

'Thank you,' I said. 'It's all new to me, I must see how it goes.'

He went down the hall swinging his cane. As far as I know he's been out of work the whole five or six years he's been my neighbour. He keeps so fit that it's hard to tell how old he is but by the brightness of his eye I'd say he's at least fifty-five. Most of the voices I hear through the wall belong to young men of the antique-shop type but I think he lives off old ladies. I've no reason to think it except his looks. His eyes look as if he's pawned his real ones and is wearing paste.

After I'd set up the aquarium I looked in my book of Bewick engravings for an oyster-catcher but couldn't find one. Bewick has drawn the dotterel, the spotted redshank, the godwit and the little stint but there's no oyster-catcher in my book. He would have drawn it very well, it's his sort of bird. The best bird drawings I've done were for *Delia Swallow's Housewarming*, one of my early books. The story was rubbish but the swallow was well observed, she was a distinct Laura Ashley type.

3

William G.

It must have been soft plastic, that gorilla the little boy had. I don't think they make those things out of rubber any more.

There are green turtles whose feeding grounds are along the coast of Brazil, and they swim 1,400 miles to breed and lay their eggs on Ascension Island in the South Atlantic, half way to Africa. Ascension Island is only five miles long. Nobody knows how they find it. Two of the turtles at the Aquarium are green turtles, a large one and a small one. The sign said: 'The Green Turtle, *Chelonia mydas*, is the source of turtle soup ... ' I am the source of William G. soup if it comes to that. Everyone is the source of his or her kind of soup. In a town as big as London that's a lot of soup walking about.

How do the turtles find Ascension Island? There are sharks in the water too. Some of the turtles get eaten by sharks. Do the turtles know about sharks? How do they not think about the sharks when they're swimming that 1,400 miles? Green turtles must have the kind of mind that doesn't think about sharks unless a shark is there. That must be how it is with them. I can't believe they'd swim 1,400 miles thinking about sharks. Sea turtles can't shut themselves up in their shells as land turtles do. Their shells are like tight bone vests and their flippers are always sticking out. Nothing they can do if a shark comes along. Pray. Ridiculous to think of a turtle praying with all those teeth coming up from below.

Mr Meager, manager of the shop and the source of Meager soup, stood in front of me for a while. When I noticed him he asked me if I'd got something on my mind. Green turtles, I said. Was that something we'd subscribed, he wanted to know. No, I said, it was the source of turtle soup. He went away with a hard smile.

It's hard to believe they do it by observing the angle of the sun like a yachtsman with a sextant. Carr doubts it and he's about the biggest turtle authority there is. But that's what penguins do on overland journeys. They're big navigators too. I think of the turtles swimming steadily against the current all the way to Ascension. I think of them swimming through all that golden-green water over the dark, over the chill of the deeps and the jaws of the dark. And I think of the sun over the water, the sun through the water, the eye holding the sun, being held by it with no thought and only the rhythm of the going, the steady wing-strokes of the flippers in the water. Then it doesn't seem hard to believe. It seems the only way to do it, the only way in fact to be: swimming, swimming, the eye held by the sun, no sharks in the mind, nothing in the mind. And when they can't see the sun, what then? Their vision isn't good enough for star sights. Do they go by smell, taste, faith?

In the evening I went downstairs for a cup of tea with Mrs Inchcliff, my landlady. She wasn't in the kitchen, I found her in the lumber-room. Her boyfriend Charlie when he lived here used to spend a lot of time in that room. There's a workbench there and she was sitting on it under a green-shaded light with her feet on a saw-horse. She's sixty years old, still a good-looking woman, must have been beautiful when she was younger. Goes about in jeans and shirts and sandals mostly, wears her hair long. From the back she looks like a girl except that her hair is grey.

'With just a little more capital Charlie and I could have made a go of the antique shop,' she said. 'If we could have hung on for another year we'd have been all right. Charlie loved it.'

Charlie had indeed been very good at finding things, stripping off paint and varnish, rebuilding and restoring. He was twenty-five when they broke up a couple of years ago. He went off with a woman of fifty who had a stall on the Portobello Road.

When he and Mrs Inchcliff had been in business a good many of their antiques had cost them nothing at all. They used to go out scavenging in her old estate-car almost every day. They'd had a regular route of rubbish tips and she still kept her hand in. When a building was due to be condemned she usually beat everyone else to the knocker on the front door and she seemed to find the most profitable skips on both sides of the river. She was always shifting odd doors and dressers and various scraps of timber and ironmongery, more out of habit than anything else though I daresay she made a few pounds a week selling things to dealers.

'If you ever want to do any woodworking,' she said, 'shelves or anything, you can use the tools and everything here whenever you like.' She's said that to me several times.

'Thanks,' I said. 'There's nothing I need to make right now.' When I had a house I used to make things. When I had a family. When the girls sat on my lap and I read to them.

I sat down on a chest. There was a sack trolley leaning in the corner, left over from the antique-shop days. I saw myself walking down a dark street in the middle of the night wheeling a turtle on the sack trolley. Just a flash and it was gone. There was a pebble in the pocket of my cardigan, left there from the last time I stopped smoking. From the beach at Antibes. Look, Dad, here's a good one. It was cool and smooth between my fingers.

'I wonder what Charlie's doing now,' said Mrs Inch-cliff.

There must be a lot of people in the world being wondered about by people who don't see them any more.

4

Neaera H.

I don't think I've ever seen anyone pick up a box of matches without shaking it. Curious. It takes more time to shake the box than it would to open it straight away but it's less effort. It's pleasant to hear a lot of matches rattling in the box, one has a feeling of plenty. No one wants to open a matchbox and find it empty.

I lit a cigarette and looked at the water-beetle parcel. A nice little brown-paper parcel, short and cylindrical with airholes in the top. When I undid the brown paper there was a nice little tin with airholes in the lid. Inside the tin was the beetle on damp moss. It was a female, I could tell by the ridges on the wing covers. No males available, said the invoice taped to the tin. That's life.

With a pencil I prodded her into the little net I'd bought, then lifted the aquarium cover and put her into the water. She swam right down to the plastic shipwreck and scuttled out of sight inside it.

One of my books quoted a naturalist who'd kept a water-beetle on raw meat for three and a half years. I dropped some raw meat through the feeding hole. The beetle rushed over to it, flung it about a bit, then left it and moored herself to a water plant.

Something will come to me, I thought. *Delia Beetle's Sunken Treasure*. No, I used that name for the swallow. Cynthia Beetle, Sally Beetle, Victoria Beetle.

Victoria Beetle, Secret Agent. A woman of action. I went out and sat in the square.

There is no statue in our square. When I look at statues I find later that I have usually not paid close attention but I have paid close attention to the statue that is not in our square. I've come to think of it as a fountain really. There's a large stone basin and a little thin bronze girl with her skirt tucked up, paddling in the water. She's not in the centre of the basin but near the rim. In the centre there's a little jet of water that shoots up taller than the girl. Sometimes the wind blows drops of water spattering on the girl. When it rains, the water in the basin is spangled with splashes that leap up to meet the rain. The bronze girl gleams in the rain. When the sun shines her shadow moves over the water, over the stone rim, over the paving round the fountain. The bronze girl is always at the centre of the circle of her revolving shadow that marks the time.

In Sloane Square there really is a fountain. With two basins and a proper fountain lady in the upper basin pouring water from a shell, a kneeling bronze physical-education sort of lady, naked but unapproachable. I think of her name as being Daphne. Sometimes an empty Coca-Cola tin, bright and shining, circles her basin like part of a water clock. But that bronze lady and her fountain are cold and heavy compared to the statue and the fountain that are not in our square. There would be beach pebbles in the basin of the bronze-girl fountain.

Having reviewed my customary fountain thoughts I find all at once that I really don't care about it at all. Let the square be however it is, it doesn't matter to me any more.

I have only one beach pebble from my childhood, from Caister. I don't suppose it makes any difference, the others are always there in a way. The books call them pebbles but I always think of them as stones. I have many stones from beaches I've visited as a grown-up, one bit of sea-china with a voluptuous fairy with little butterfly wings on it, and several bits of sea-glass. The stones from each place are in separate baskets: St David's head, Folkestone, Staunton Sands etc. At Folkestone I gave a talk to teachers and librarians one evening, and in the afternoon of that day I went to the sea front and down steep steps to the narrow pebble beach and the sea.

There was a long row of little beach-huts side by side like garages. It was a rainy day in early spring. A man had his hut opened up, the whole front open like a dolls' house. He was doing the sort of things men do when they smoke pipes and repair their boats in early spring. Mending something I suppose. There was no boat, his hut was his boat. All the little beach-hut fronts pushed me towards the sea and I jumped down from the wall on to the pebbles that rolled and clicked under me as I walked. I thought: what if there were a stone with my name on it? Then I thought, what if my name were on every stone? Then: the name of every stone is in me. I can't say the name of every stone but it is in me. There were no birds that I remember that day. The hotels along the front were as high as in childhood and as remote, even when seen close to.

This afternoon I bought a marked-down bird book with plates by John Gould (1804–1881). There's a handsome picture of two oyster-catchers. 'At running, diving, and swimming they are unrivalled, while their vigilance is greatly appreciated by the other birds of the shore,' says the book. The newer bird books have hundreds of posh pictures, the proficiency of the artists is dazzling. But the birds all look as if they'd been done from photographs. Certainly there were no such bird pictures before the camera came into use. Gould's birds are beautiful but modestly done and he seems to have looked at each one carefully and long. His eagle owl, *Bubo bubo*, is all ferocity but without malice. Dangling from his beak is a dead rabbit who looks exactly like Peter Rabbit without the blue jacket. *Bubo bubo*'s dreadful amber eyes say simply, 'It has fallen to me to do this. It is my lot.' His fierce woolly owl-babies huddle before him waiting for their dinner.

5

William G.

I went to the Zoo again.

Cold day. Windy. Walking down Parkway from the Camden Town tube station I passed a girl with her anorak zipped up pushing a baby in a push-chair, looking cold. Autumn? No, spring. Summer next. Four seasons to a year. I can easily imagine getting up one morning and deciding not to bother with any more seasons. I went in by the South Gate and passed the Waders Aviary on my way to the sea turtles.

Lots of noise from the reeds and marsh plants inside the cage. More than one voice, some sort of a controversy: kleep kleep kleep. Kleep kleep. Two black-and-white birds with orange-ringed eyes set neatly in their heads, long orange bills and the sort of chilblained but durable-looking purplish legs one sees on some lady birdwatchers. But these birds were both men I think. Maybe it was one bird and a doppel-ganger. They were walking side by side shouting at each other. They passed out of view behind the reeds. I went round to the other side of the cage where I could see them as they came out on to the concrete beach round their wading-pool. They were walking with their heads down and if they'd had hands they would have had them clasped behind their backs. Each one's bill was pointed down and away from the other and they looked stubbornly sideways at each other as they conversed.

'Kleep it and have klept with it for God's sake,' said one.

'I don't have to kleep it just because you klawp I should,' said the other.

'Then don't kleep it,' said the first one. 'It's no klank off my klonk.'

'Oh aye,' said the second one. 'You klawp that now but that's not what you klawped a little klink ago.'

'I klick very klenk what I klawped a little klink ago,' said the first one. 'I klawped either kleep it or don't kleep it but stop klawping about it. That's what I klawped.'

'It's all very klenk for you to klawp "Kleep it," ' said the second one. 'You're not the one that has to kleggy back the kwonk.'

I didn't want to hear any more. There was a sign inside the cage with pictures of the inmates. Those two were oyster-catchers. That's a laugh. I'd like to know when the last time they caught an oyster was. At one end of their pool, which was nothing more than a depression in the concrete with some standing water in it, some very old mussels were lying about. There were other birds with their pictures on the sign but I didn't want to know.

Have the gibbons been corrupted by captivity? How can they possibly be happy in a cage, but they seem not to care about it especially. Debonair is the only word for them. Maybe aerial acrobatics are to them what jazz is to musicians who do it wherever they are and whether they get paid or not, just for the thing itself.

They have quite a large sort of flight cage with transverse bars at regular intervals for them to swing on. They saunter through the air in great long easy arcs, long arms revolving alternately: catch, let go, catch, let go, and all the time not particularly paying attention and as if with their hands in their pockets. Their manner is cool but lively, not withdrawn. Their small black faces are full of Zen. Jazz acrobats is what they are and they seem philosophically beyond such trifles as a cage. They're above me, I admit it. And they don't seem to be snobs about it either.

I had sort of a bursting feeling as if my self were a wall round me that I couldn't knock down or climb over. I have no talent, no Zen like that of the gibbons. Once, twice, long ago. Out of it, away and in the clear. What's the use of remembering. Out of it was at the same time into it. There's a wall inside the self as well. Can't get through any more. Can't live is what it amounts to. No place to live. Get through the days, the seasons, oh yes. But no place to be. No way to hold the sun in the eye, be held by it swimming, swimming.

The wax people downstairs at Madame Tussaud's contemplating in wax their crimes get through the days, the nights, the seasons. The thought escapes me, there was more to it. Prisons are all we know how to make, even in wax. No wax sea turtles, thank God for that.

There they were in the golden-green murk of their little box of sea, their little bedsitter of ocean. One almost expected a meter in the corner of it where they had to put in 5p to keep the water circulating. Thousands of miles in their speechless eyes, submarine skies in their flipper-wings. No beach of course, no hot sand for the gravid females to crawl up on to, to lay their eggs.

A little boy pointed to the big loggerhead turtle. 'Could he get rid of me?' he said to his mother. She was ever so well-groomed.

'Oh no,' she said, laughing upper-class and mumsily. 'They're quite harmless.'

The male loggerhead bit the female on the neck and tried to mount her. Not on. She wasn't having any. Maybe the females in the Aquarium don't get gravid, have no eggs to lay. The lady walked away with her knickers full of gentility, her son followed, still not got rid of.

Thousands of miles of navigation, I couldn't get it out of my mind. There was a girl standing next to me, a burstly sort of girl, bursting out of her tight trousers and blouse, bursting with health and burstly genes. *She'd* have no trouble getting gravid whenever she liked. I was still thinking of the thousands of miles. 'Nobody knows how they do it,' I said.

'You just have to be here at the right time and you can see them do it,' she said. Burst burst.

The air seemed full of noise, I sat down on a bench and closed my eyes, saw golden-green water, thousands of miles.

6

Neaera H.

Madame Beetle seems not to fancy raw meat. All of what I'd given her lay about in the plants and on the shipwreck and went white and sodden. On the other hand, maybe she *has* eaten it. In the larval stage the water-beetle doesn't eat in the ordinary way, it injects digestive fluid into its prey and sucks out the liquefied tissues. Maybe Madame Beetle's never grown up. The meat certainly looks as if there's no nutrition left in it. I tried her with a bit of braised beef and I think she ate some of it.

She spends a good deal of her time hanging head-down with her bottom just breaking the surface of the water. That's the end she breathes through, where her spiracles are. Might she have a periscope? *Victoria Beetle, Submariner*. When she dives she takes a shining bubble of air with her under her wing-covers. If I took the lid off the tank and opened the window she might fly away but it would be a long trip to the nearest pond. I sometimes think of her as waiting patiently but I doubt that she really experiences what people call waiting and if she doesn't then she has no need of patience.

Victoria Beetle's Summer Holiday. Bugger that. *Sunken Treasure* is better. What would a beetle treasure be? I'll try catching some flies for her. Maybe a moth will turn up, she'd like that. But the treasure in the story should be jewels or money.

It was a lazy summer afternoon,
and Victoria Beetle was enjoying a quiet cup of tea
when she heard a knock at the door.
She looked out of the window
and saw Big Sam Bumblebee the gang boss.
'If he thinks he can try on that
protection lark with me he'd better think again,'
said Victoria, and she picked up the poker.

Victoria Beetle or Victoria Water-Beetle? The hyphenated name sounds better. How would Snugg & Sharpe feel about gangsters? After all they're part of modern life even at schools nowadays, according to the newspapers. Big Sam knows where the lolly is but he needs Victoria's help because it's at the bottom of the pond. Dropped there by Jimson Crow perhaps, whilst making a getaway. He's always stealing things. He was flying over the pond with Detective Owl hot on his trail.

I wanted to see an oyster-catcher so I went to the Zoo, not feeling at all good about it. The Zoo is a prison for animals who have been sentenced without trial and I feel guilty because I do nothing about it. But there it was, I wanted to see an oyster-catcher and I was no better than the people who'd caged oyster-catchers for me to see. And I myself have caged a water-beetle. On the other hand perhaps some of the birds and animals don't feel the Zoo to be a prison. Maybe they've been corrupted by it.

At the Waders Aviary a little sandpiper who would never have allowed me to come that close in real life perched on a sign a foot away from me and stared. He knew that he was safe because the wire mesh of the cage was between us. He has lost his innocence. He appeared to have lost a leg as well, and for a long time stood steadfastly on the one very slender remaining member whilst looking at me through half-closed eyes. Having kept me there for nearly half an hour he revealed a second leg that matched the other perfectly, then flew down to the sand and entertained a lady sandpiper with an elegant little dance that seemed done less for the lady than for the thing itself. He made his legs even longer and thinner than they were, drew himself up quite tall in his small way, spread his wings, wound himself up and produced a noise like a tiny paddle-wheel boat whilst flapping his wings stiffly and with formal regularity. At the same time he executed some very subtle steps almost absent-mindedly, with the air of one who could be blindingly nimble if he let himself go. The lady watched attentively. At a certain point, as if by mutual agreement that the proprieties had been observed, he stopped dancing, she stopped watching. They went their separate ways like two people at a cocktail party.

Oyster-catchers were what I'd come to see and there were two or three of them mooching about but there was something wrong that made the seeing of them flat and uneventful. I'd never been that close to them before, part of their character had been that they were always seen from a distance on the open mudflats with a wide and low horizon far away. These oyster-catchers were so accessible as to be unobservable. One of them wound himself up as the sandpiper had done and released quite an urgent kleep kleep kleep. The sound independently hurried off round the pool and the bird hurried after it like a cat or a child working up interest in a toy. When the sound stopped the oyster-catcher abandoned it and began to potter about with some rather old-looking mussels.

There were all sorts of waders in the Waders Aviary, not all of whom would ordinarily have been seen in the same place I think. The sign showed pictures of a red-shank, guillemot, razorbill, eider duck, oyster-catcher, ruff, kittiwake, white-breasted waterhen, rufous laughing thrush, curlew, laysan duck and hooded merganser. They had their concrete pool to wade in, they had reeds and bushes and a strip of sand. The Zoological Society had pieced together a habitat that was like the little naif towns one sometimes sees in model railway lay-outs. The elements of it were thing for thing a rough approximation of reality but the scale wasn't right and the parts of it didn't fit together in a realistic way.

The birds were all quite good-natured and reason-able about it, they seemed more grown-up than the Zoo management, as if they'd been caught and caged not because they weren't clever enough to avoid it but be-cause they simply didn't think in terms of nets and cages, those were things for cunning children. So here they all were, interned for none of them knew how long. They made the best of it better than people would have done I think, and all of them appeared to get on rather neatly together. The sandpipers, the curlews and the redshanks, all pure Bewick, seemed to draw serenity from the sheer detail of their markings. A ruff was bathing with its ruff spread out as large as possible. It looked of the film world and as if it might call everyone 'Darling'.

I felt dissatisfied, as one does when morally strong preconceptions have to be questioned. The birds were not silent prisoners wasting away like Dr Manette in the Bastille nor were they beating pitiful wings against the wire mesh of their captivity. Their understanding of the whole thing seemed deeper and simpler than mine. Of course it may be that they're going decadent. I've seen a film in which Dr Lorenz pointed out the differences between two colonies of cattle egrets, one free and one caged. The free ones, who had to provide for themselves, were monogamous and energetic and kept their numbers within ecologically reasonable limits. The captive egrets were promiscuous, idle, overbreeding and presumably going to hell fast.

I passed the gibbons who seemed at the same time active and reflective, of more mature understanding than the party of French girls who stood before the cage shouting, 'Allez, allez!' at their aerial artistry. I avoided the lions, the rhinoceroses and the elephants, walked along with my head down, not wanting to see anything and not wanting to go home. I fetched up at the Aquarium as it began to rain, and went inside.

Aquaria have always been interesting to me as sources of illumination, the fish are secondary. Madame Beetle's tank with its sunken wreck, water plants, pebbles and one bit of sea-china is very pretty when lit in the evening. Madame Beetle is more active than she was at first, submarining elegantly, her red fringed hind legs going like perfectly co-ordinated oars. I like the sound of the pump and filter too, it's better than the ticking of a clock.

When I was a child I had a fishless aquarium. My father set it up for me with gravel and plants and pebbles before he'd got the fish and I asked him to leave it as it was for a while. The pump kept up a charming burble, the green-gold light was wondrous when the room was dark. I put in a china mermaid and a tin horseman who maintained a relationship like that of the figures on Keats's Grecian urn except that the horseman grew rusty. Eventually fish were pressed upon me and they seemed an intrusion, I gave them to a friend. All that aquarium wanted was the sound of the pump, the gently waving plants, the mysterious pebbles and the silent horseman forever galloping to the mermaid smiling in the green-gold light. I used to sit and look at them for hours. The mermaid and the horseman were from my father. I have them in a box somewhere, I'm not yet ready to take them out and look at them again.

Here in the dark of the Aquarium were many green-and-gold-lit windows, huge compared to mine but not magical. The fish all looked bored to death but of course fish aren't meant to be looked at closely, will not bear close examination. The lobsters scarcely looked more alive than those I've seen waiting to be selected by diners at sea-food restaurants. I don't think the Aquarium ought to do a shark at all if they're not going to lay on a big one. The leopard shark they have is so small that his vacant stare and receding chin make him seem nothing more than a marine form of twit rather than a representative of a mortally dangerous species. Rays I think ought not to be seen at all outside their natural habitat, too many questions arise.

I'd been aware of the turtles for some time before I went to look at them. I knew I'd have to do it but I kept putting it off. When I did go to see them I didn't know how to cope with it. Untenable propositions assembled themselves in my mind. If these were what they were then why were buildings, buses, streets? The sign said that green turtles were the source of turtle soup and hawksbills provided the tortoise-shell of commerce. But why soup, why spectacles?

Relative to her size my beetle has more than twice as much swimming-room as the turtles. And in that little tank the turtles were flying, flying in the water, submarine albatrosses. I've read about them, they navigate hundreds of miles of ocean. I imagined a sledge-hammer smashing the thick glass, letting out the turtles and their little bit of ocean, but then they'd only be flopping about on the wet floor.

I'm always afraid of being lost, the secret navigational art of the turtles seems a sacred thing to me. I thought of the little port of Polperro in Cornwall where they sell sea-urchin lamps, then I felt very sad and went home.

7

William G.

What a weird thing smoking is and I can't stop it. I feel cosy, have a sense of well-being when I'm smoking, poisoning myself, killing myself slowly. Not so slowly maybe. I have all kinds of pains I don't want to know about and I know that's what they're from. But when I don't smoke I scarcely feel as if I'm living. I don't feel as if I'm living unless I'm killing myself. Very good. Wonderful.

One time I grew a beard. I didn't want to see my face in the mirror any more while shaving so I stopped shaving. I'd already stopped looking at myself when brushing my teeth and washing my face and I used to comb my hair without a mirror, feeling the parting with my fingers. It was a relief at first but when the beard reached a state of full growth I was constantly aware of walking around behind it so I got rid of it. Since then I've had to see my face almost every morning. I don't shave on my Saturdays off nor on Sundays unless I'm going out in the evening.

I used to think when I shaved and looked at my face that that bit of time didn't count, was just the time in between things. Now I think it's the time that counts most. It's those times that all the other times are in between. It's the time when nothing helps and the great heavy boot of the past is planted squarely in your back and shoving you forward. Sometimes my mind gives me a flash of road I'll never see again, sometimes a face that's gone, gone. Moments like grains of sand but the beach is empty. Millions of moments in forty-five years. Letters in boxes, photos in drawers.

So breakfast is a useful thing, a rallying point for all the members of me. We all sit together at the table by the window to start the day off. My face comes along as well. Breakfast is always the same, perfectly reliable, no decisions, no conflicts: orange juice, muesli, a three-minute boiled egg, a slice of buttered toast, coffee that I grind myself.

There's a tiny kitchen on the landing just outside my door, a cooker and a little fridge and a sink. Mr Sandor uses it before me in the morning, Miss Neap comes after me. Mr Sandor always leaves the cooker sticky and smelling heavily organic. I don't know what he has for breakfast. Squid maybe. Kelp. Nasty-looking little parcels in the fridge. I always leave the cooker clean for Miss Neap. I could have a word with Sandor about it but cleaning the cooker seems less tiresome. The problem only arises in the mornings. Even on weekends he always has lunch and supper out. Once I attempted a conversation with the man and he waved a foreign newspaper about and grunted something through his heavy moustache about scoundrels in government. He seems violent and heavily burdened with thoughts of whatever country the newspaper is from. He carries a briefcase, the kind that looks as if it might be full of sausages. I've no idea what he does for a living. Miss Neap works at a theatre-ticket agency and visits her mother in Leeds some weekends. Her hair is that kind of blonde that only happens after fifty, she wears a pince-nez and a tightly-belted leopardskin coat and has blue eyes like ice. If Sandor breakfasted after me and before her I think he'd leave the cooker clean.

The sea turtles are on my mind all the time. I can feel something building up in me, feel myself becoming strange and unsafe. Today one of those women who never know titles came into the shop. They are the source of Knightsbridge lady soup and they ask for a good book for a nephew or something new on roses for a gardening husband. This one wanted a novel, 'something for a good read at the cottage'. I offered her *Procurer to the King* by Fallopia Bothways. Going like a bomb with the menopausal set. She gasped, and I realized I'd actually spoken the thought aloud: 'Going like a bomb with the menopausal set.'

She went quite red. 'What did you say?' she said.

'Going like a bomb, it's the best she's written yet,' I said, and looked very dim.

She let it pass, settled on *Lances of Glory* by Taura Strong and did not complain to Mr Meager about me, which was really quite decent of her. But I have to be careful.

Every evening a lady and her husband and their greyhound bitch go slowly past the house. The husband and wife must be in their early sixties and the greyhound isn't young. The husband drags one leg and when the windows are open I can always hear them coming and know who it is even if I don't look out. They walk on opposite sides of the street, wife and greyhound on one side, husband on the other. The husband works for London Transport I think. Why a greyhound? Perhaps it's a retired racer. The street is very narrow and so are the pavements, which may explain why they walk on opposite sides although I've seen other couples walk side by side. Perhaps he needs more space around him because of his bad leg. The greyhound of course walks very slowly too, as if she's forgotten any other way of going. When I see them in the evening slowly passing by they look larger than life and allegorical.

The Underground trains are above ground where the District Line passes the common. On the right the tracks disappear behind a wall, on the left they converge towards Parsons Green and Putney Bridge. I watch the trains a lot. There are six lights on the front of each train, two vertical rows of three, and the pattern in which some are lit and some are dark tells the destination. For Special trains all six are lit. Three on the left and the bottom one on the right say Upminster, and so forth. There's a little sign as well that says where they're going. By watching with binoculars I've learnt most of the light code, I still don't know all of the signals. I rather like seeing the lights pass in the dark and thinking: Tower Hill or whatever. Sometimes I look at the empty tracks with my binoculars. The solid grey iron is peculiarly pleasing to the eye, the coloured lights almost taste red and green in the mouth. I used to go birdwatching with the binoculars. Sometimes I hear an owl on the common.

Weekends are dicey. Saturdays aren't too bad, there's the shop to go to or errands to do and lots of people on the street, football crowds in the afternoon. Sundays are dangerous, the quiet waits in ambush. Close the museums and there's no telling what might happen.

Saturday afternoon I did not go to the Zoo, I went to the National Maritime Museum at Greenwich to look at Port Liberty.

8

Neaera H.

There is a connection between my turtle thoughts and my Polperro thoughts but I'm not sure I can find it. Polperro is mentioned in the guide-books as one of the prettiest fishing villages on the Cornish coast. I'd never seen it until last spring when I was visiting friends in Devon. We drove along many narrow roads winding between hedgerows, crossed the Tamar Bridge into Cornwall, passed through Looe and arrived at a car-park. Near it was a whitewashed inn on which was mounted a millwheel smartly painted black and slowly revolving. I don't remember seeing any stream to turn the wheel, I have the impression that a little gush of water had been piped in for that purpose.

One of the principal industries in Polperro is parking cars. We parked, then joined many people walking slowly through the narrow streets eating ice-cream, leading, pushing and carrying infants and scowling at such cars as had not parked. There were many post-cards, many sea-urchins, many pottery things and shiny coppery things for sale, many Cream Teas. There was a model village, the entrance to which was through an orange-lit souvenir shop with music. We passed through the souvenirs, the orange light and the music as under a waterfall, paid 10p and came out into what must have been the garden once and was now the model village.

There was organ music, very reduced and scant-sounding, playing *Abide with Me*. I guessed it was coming from the model church and I was right. The model village was Polperro itself, as could be observed by looking over a low wall towards the real street. There one saw a full-size sign that said GARNER and next to it the Claremont Hotel, then looking down saw the miniature GARNER and the Claremont Hotel, lumpish and simplified in the model.

The model houses and shops, thick and awry, had an air of stolid outrage. It was as if the anima of each place, private and indwelling, had been nagged into standing naked in the little streets before the deformed buildings. As if someone had said, 'We need the money, you must help.' The very boats in the model harbour, oafish and out of scale in the still water, cursed almost aloud, denied any connection whatever with real boats, fishing and the sea, tried by dissociating themselves to make amends to the poor household gods of the port.

A large orange tiger cat settled comfortably on one of the model roofs and a black-and-white cat picked its way through the streets as if looking out for model sinners on a model Day of Judgment. There were pence and halfpence on the bottom of the model harbour. People do that everywhere in fountains I know. Is it possible that they made wishes here when they threw in their coins?

We emerged, went on past Cream Teas and sea-urchins to the full-size harbour, a small one sheltered by a breakwater. The fishing boats were few, there was one called *Ocean Gift*. A young woman with a Polaroid camera repeatedly photographed her bald baby who had the face of a mature publican, showing him the picture each time. Gulls with cruel yellow

37

eyes paced the quay. A jackdaw perched on the sea wall, neat, detached, seeming full of critical comment but saying nothing. There was a sign at the harbour which I copied:

POLPERRO HARBOUR
Polperro is the best example
of the
small Cornish fishing ports
and the Harbour Trustees
are anxious to retain
its character without resorting
to commercialization
The cost of maintenance
far exceeds the income
WILL YOU PLEASE HELP?

There was a box with a slot. A few feet away were a souvenir stand and a shop full of pottery things and coppery things and sea-urchin lamps with light bulbs in them shining through the sea-urchins. I put no money in the box. Polperro seemed to me like a street-walker asking for money to maintain her virginity.

The tide hadn't come all the way in and there was a patch of dry stony beach on the seaward side of the wall. I went down the steps and walked there. The beach offered little more than broken glass and contra-ceptives. At least there was some vitality left here I thought. I contented myself with two stones and three lumps of glass and a bit of china worn smooth. As we left the harbour I saw a boat lying on the mud. It was full of loose planks and had a hole in its side. Someone had lettered SHIT on it with a paint brush.

Would it be just as well for Polperro to break up its boats and pave its harbour for a car-park? But of course without the harbour and the token boats no one would come to park there. If the turtles were set free, where is there for them to go really? To what can they navigate? They swim hundreds of miles to the beaches of their breeding grounds. The hundred eggs the female lays each time are just barely enough to ensure the race against wild dogs and predatory birds on the beaches, sharks in the water. I've read in Carr that wild dogs from far away travel to the beaches to wait for the arrival of the turtles. Still the hundred eggs would be enough, but nothing ensures the turtles against the manufacturers of turtle soup. Three-hundred pound turtles navigate the ocean and come ashore to be slaughtered for the five pounds of cartilage that gets sold to the soup-makers. They're torn open and mutilated, left belly-up and dead or dying on the beach.

Is my wanting to set the Zoo turtles free a kind of Polperrization, a trying to pretend that something is when it isn't? Would they have to swim with signs and slotted boxes begging for protection and support? There's rubbish in the oceans now far from any land, Coca-Cola tins perhaps circling among the icebergs. If turtles have memories the beaches the old ones remember are not what they would find now. Perhaps the only decent thing would be a monster Turtle-arium charging a proper admission, with turtle rides 10p and YOUR PHOTO WITH A SEA TURTLE 50p. Something has got to be whole in some way but my mind isn't strong enough to work it out. Carr's turtle station at Tortuguero in Costa Rica sounds a lovely place in his book. It sounds the sort of place where at night if you looked through the palm trees there'd always be lights on and coffee and people with clipboards. Tortuguero. The name sounds like hot sun, blue water, white surf.

Often in the evenings Madame Beetle hangs head-down in the water cleaning her legs with great diligence like a woman really looking after herself. She seems to have settled in quite nicely, has a good appetite. She attacks the raw meat vigorously when I drop it in, then hangs head-down holding it in her front legs while her mandibles are busy with it. I don't know whether any of the meat actually disappears, there's always a good deal of it about that goes white and filmy after a while, but she must get something out of it because she's still alive. I remove the old bits from the tank with a skewer. When I first took the cover off to do that I thought Madame Beetle might fly away but she simply retired inside the shipwreck until I'd finished.

I've bought a little china figure, a bathing beauty in a 1900s mauve bathing-suit and cap, red bathing-slippers. She's sitting on a rock leaning back on her elbows, her right knee raised and her right ankle resting on her left knee. Her pretty rosy-cheeked face is turned to the side and as she sits before the aquarium on my desk she looks as if she's been watching Madame Beetle and has just turned away towards me. Possibly there's a story in her as well. Possibly there's no story either in her or Madame Beetle. It may happen to me at any time that everything will be just what it is, with no stories in anything.

9

William G.

Briefcases. Businessmen, barristers carry briefs. When I was in advertising we always talked about what our brief was. *Brief* means letter in German. Brief is short. Life is a brief case. Brief candle, out, out. In the tube there was a very small, very poor-looking man in a threadbare suit and a not very clean shirt, spectacles. He made a roll-up, lit it, then took from his briefcase a great glossy brochure with glorious colour photographs of motorcycles. Many unshaven men carry briefcases. I've seen briefcases carried by men who looked as if they slept rough. Women tramps usually have carrier bags, plastic ones often. I carry one of those expanding files with a flap. Paper in it for taking notes, a book sometimes, sandwich and an apple for lunch. The apple bulges, can't be helped.

I took the tube to Surrey Docks, the 70 bus from there. There were some children on the bus singing *Oranges and Lemons* and they seemed to spin it out very slowly. I found myself waiting, waiting for 'Here comes a chopper to chop off your head, chop, chop, chop!' which arrived in due course and very loudly.

At Greenwich I went straight to the Port Liberty model after the guards at the door had looked into my envelope and found no bombs. They have to take precautions, that's understandable. A place like Greenwich is a temptation. The greenness and the stillness, the augustness of the buildings and the observatory dome almost make one want to set off a bomb just out of respect.

There seem to be more children than there used to be. Always lots of them about even on school days. Children seem to be the permanent population while adults drift in and out and fall away. Each year the schoolgirls in their white knee-socks seem more erotic, more secretly knowing, one thinks probably nothing would surprise them. There are always children at the Port Liberty windows. I looked over the shoulder of a girl who must have been about twelve, the scent of her hair was in my nostrils. I don't know where my daughters are now. I don't know if Dora's remarried. Someone pressed the button and the three-minute sequence began. The model sky grew slowly dark. Such a perfect world, so small and yet so full of distance. A long time ago I copied the signs that tell about Port Liberty:

APPROACHING PORT LIBERTY BY NIGHT

When night falls the navigator has to rely on the navigation lights shown by other vessels to avoid colliding with them and the lights shown by buoys, beacons and lighthouses to keep him in safe waters.

A confusion of fixed and flashing lights confronts him when he approaches a port but trained to interpret the various light colours and sequences in conjunction with his chart he can safely identify and follow the correct channel into port.

What you can see

The lighthouse on Patrol Point, whose white light is visible 20 miles out at sea, occults once every 30 seconds, while dead ahead can be seen the white light of the Landfall buoy, flashing every second.

A steady red light over a steady white light near the Landfall buoy identifies the pilot launch waiting for our arrival with a pilot ready to board and assist us through the channel to the anchorage.

The white masthead lights and green starboard navigating lights of a large vessel can be seen moving down the main channel, while the navigation lights of a smaller ship are visible coming out through the secondary channel.

Three white lights in a vertical triangle indicate a dredger working at the inner end of Crushers Bank and that it is safe to pass on either side of her.

The masthead light and port and starboard lights of a small craft off our starboard bow indicate that she is heading towards us.

The edges of the main channel are marked by the flashing lights of buoys, and further up the river the lights of fixed beacons can be discerned which assist the navigator to keep in the deeper water.

Model made to the requirements of the Department of Navigation by Thorp Modelmakers Ltd.

There were the lights fixed and flashing, each in its proper place in that perfect night miniature and vast. Then the night faded, there was sunlight on the distant hills of the port, sunlight on the water before me and on the vessels coming and going, and I was:

APPROACHING PORT LIBERTY BY DAY

When a ship approaches port the navigator has various aids to help him.

He has a chart of the area, which he keeps up to date by Admiralty Notices to Mariners, issued weekly.

He has leading marks and the international system of buoys and beacons which mark the channel which he will have to follow and which he has to look out for as he approaches.

In most ships he usually has an echo sounder to indicate to him the depth of water and a radar set to supplement his eyes if visibility is poor because of fog or rain or falling snow.

What you can see

Imagine you are standing on the navigating bridge of a ship approaching the estuary of the River Line and Port Liberty.

The Landfall buoy marking the entrance to the channel is right ahead of you and close by you can see the pilot launch displaying its distinguishing code flag waiting to put a pilot on board.

Steaming out through the main channel is a 12,000 ton cargo vessel and astern of her a coaster is about to pass through the secondary channel used by smaller craft.

There is a fishing boat heading out to sea off Plushers Point and at the inner end of Crusher's Bank a dredger is working.

Port Liberty can just be seen around the bend in the river and the buoys marking the main and secondary channels into the River Line and up to the quay are clearly visible.

Model made to the requirements of the Department of Navigation by Thorp Modelmakers Ltd.

So clear and sharp, Port Liberty. So precise and real. Realer than anything else I know. Of course it doesn't exist. There's no such place. There is no River Line, no Crusher's Bank, no Plushers Point, no Port Liberty. The chart and the soundings, the channel markers and the buoys have no counterparts in the full-size world. Port Liberty is a fiction invented by the Admiralty as Fig. 67 in the *Admiralty Manual of Navigation Volume I*, and the National Maritime Museum commissioned a model of it.

There's more to the model than meets the eye. I once got in touch with Thorp Modelmakers Ltd and was astonished to find that the tiny fixed and flashing lights are not actually on the tiny vessels, the lighthouse, the buoys. I couldn't believe it. The scale was too small for that, I was told. The lights are underneath the model and there is a system of mirrors derived from an old theatrical illusion called 'Pepper's Ghost'. The night window is a mirror and the lights fixed and flashing so perfectly, each in its proper place, are not in fact where one sees them. I think about it often.

✦❊❊✦

Neaera H.

I think there is less merit in Gerard Manley Hopkins's poem 'The Windhover' than there would have
been in not writing it. I think that Basho's frog that
jumped into the old pond has more falcon in it than
Hopkins's bird, simply because it has more of things-
as-they-are, which includes falcons and everything else.
'The Windhover' seems to me a wet poem and twit-
tish. But my judgment has become so subjective that
there are many things I must avoid. For some time I've
been avoiding poetry when possible but in an unthink-
ing moment I opened *The Faber Book of Modern Verse*
and there was Hopkins. Windhover is the old name for
the bird that is now called a kestrel. I've seen them
hovering over hedgerows, they don't want mannered
words but only the simplest and fewest, certainly
nothing longer than haiku and preferably no words at
all. I'm less reasonable than I was when young.

There was a kestrel a long time ago, perhaps that's
why I was so annoyed by the poem. We were lying in
a field, we looked up and opened our mouths and said
nothing.

The range of human types and actions is not terribly
wide. I have seen the same face on a titled lady and a
barmaid. And there seem to be only a few things to do
with life, in various combinations. I could not have
accepted the idea of myself as a stereotype when I was

young but I can now. I'm a more or less arty-intellec-
tual-looking lady of forty-three who is unmarried,
dresses more for style than for fashion, looks the sort
of spinster who doesn't keep cats and is not a vege-
tarian. Looks, I think, like a man's woman and hasn't
got a man. When I was a child grown-ups often told me
to smile, which I found presumptuous of them. People
still tell me that sometimes, mostly idiots at parties.

Sometimes I wonder if I ought to give up the push-
chair that I use instead of a shopping basket on wheels.
It has red and white stripes like the little tents one
sees over holes in the street. It may well be that the
same company makes both, I'd like it if they did. It
was lent me by a friend whose children have outgrown
it on the occasion of her giving me an orange tree and
I've never returned it. One sees a certain kind of poor
old person wheeling battered prams loaded with
rubbish or shabby push-chairs full of scavengings. My
push-chair is still smart however and I am not yet poor
and old.

Somehow I keep up with my work, always in arrears,
often uncertain whether I'm sleeping or waking. My
files decline gently from order to chaos, all kinds of
things are accumulating dust in the spare room. I can't
always find what I'm looking for. Easy is the slope of
Hell. I sit at the typewriter, I sit at the drawing-table,
proof copies appear from time to time, then bound
copies, so I seem to go on doing what I do. Royalty
cheques twice a year. '*Gillian Vole's Jumble Sale* was
absolutely the hit of the sales conference,' writes my
editor, 'and we expect it to do even better than *Gillian
Vole's Christmas*. Whatever Gillian is up to now, we
and all of her other fans look forward to her next
appearance.'

Well, Gillian Vole may jolly well have packed it in. I couldn't think of another Gillian Vole story right now to save my life. I've become quite fond of Madame Beetle but simply as a flatmate. Suddenly I don't know, haven't the faintest idea how people make up stories about anything. Anything is whatever it happens to be, why on earth make up stories.

At three o'clock in the morning I sat in the dark looking out of the window down at the square where the fountain is not and I thought about the turtles. The essence of it is that they can find something and they are not being allowed to do it. What more can you do to a creature, short of killing it, than prevent it from finding what it can find? How must they feel? Is there a sense in them of green ocean, white surf and hot sand? Probably not. But there *is* a drive in them to find it as they swoop in their golden-green light with their flippers clicking against the glass as they turn. Is there anything to be done about it? My mind is not an organizational one.

What is there to find? Thomas Bewick diligently followed the patterns of light from feather to feather, John Clare looked carefully at hedgerows, Emily Dickinson cauterized her lopped-off words with dashes. Ella Wheeler Wilcox implacably persisted. Shackleton came back against all odds, Scott didn't. There was a round-the-world singlehanded sailing race in which one of the yachtsmen stopped in one part of the ocean and broadcast false positions.

There is no place for me to find. No beach, no breeding grounds. Do I owe the turtles more or less because of that? Is everyone obliged to help those who have it in them to find something? I bought a second-hand mathematical book, I don't know why, on self-replicating automata. Not robots but mathematical models. The book said that random search could not account for evolution. Something evidently wants there to be finding. Time's arrow points one way only. Even the moment just past cannot be returned to.

I went into the kitchen, had some tea and toast, came back and sat in my reading chair with my eyes closed. When I opened them it was time for lunch. I had some cheese and apples, went out. I had no intention of going to the Zoo but I went there. The penguins were yawping and honking in a way that had unmistakably to do with procreation. An Australian crane was performing a remarkable dance for his mate. It was as if place and time were internalized in them and not in their surroundings, like Englishmen who dress for dinner on plantations in Borneo. The lions and tigers have no such faculty, must pace madly or lie still and doze.

I stood in the darkness by the turtle tank for some time, not so much looking at the turtles as just being near them and waiting. A man in shirt-sleeves came out of a door marked PRIVATE and stood in front of one of the fish tanks as if checking something. He was obviously one of the keepers and he had an air of decency about him, as if he paid attention to the things that really need attention paid to them.

I rehearsed the question several times in my mind, then spoke to him. 'Were any of the turtles full-grown when they were brought here?' I said.

'No,' he said. 'They were only little when they came here, no more than a pound or two. The big ones have been here twenty or thirty years.'

'Full-grown turtles,' I said, 'how are they transported?'

I I

William G.

A lady came into the shop one afternoon, arty-intellectual type about my age or a little younger. She was wearing a long orange Indian-print skirt, an old purple velvet jacket, a denim shirt and expensive boots. Not at all bad-looking. Rather troubled face, circles under her eyes. All at once I felt a strong urge to talk to her for hours and hours about everything. And at the same time I felt an urge not to talk to her at all.

She drifted about the Natural History shelves for a time in a sleepwalking sort of way, picking up books and turning the pages without always looking at them. Then she picked up a book on sea turtles by Robert Bustard and read about a quarter of it where she stood. Eerie, the way she read, as if she'd simply forgotten to put the book down. And eerie that she was reading about sea turtles. Obviously I can't be the only one thinking about them but I had the shocking feeling that here was another one of me locked up alone in a brain with the same thoughts. Me, what's that after all? An arbitrary limitation of being bounded by the people before and after and on either side. Where they leave off I begin, and vice versa. I once saw a cartoon sequence of a painter painting a very long landscape. When he'd finished he cut it up into four landscapes of the usual proportions. Mostly one doesn't meet others from the same picture. When it happens it can be unsettling

Had we anything new on sea turtles other than the Bustard, she asked. Her voice was as I expected, low and husky. She spoke as if she'd come a long way from wherever she'd been in her mind and couldn't stop long.

No, I said. Nothing else new. Had she read Carr?

Yes, she had. She looked directly at me when I mentioned Carr as if registering the fact that I knew of him. Then it seemed her mind went elsewhere, she thanked me and left the shop.

Pity, in a way. If she'd been young and pretty would I have tried to extend the conversation? Maybe. Maybe not. I don't really want to talk to a woman who's accumulated the sort of things in her head that I have in mine. And I haven't had much interest in women at all for a while, not in a realistic way. Fantasies, yes. But not actualities, not practicalities. For a time after the break-up I went to bed with as many girls as I could but nothing lasted and I didn't want it to. They wanted attention paid to them, attention paid to a present they were part of and a future that belonged to them, and my mind was elsewhere.

I used to want to find someone to listen to Chopin with. Now I don't even like to hear Chopin. Nor Scarlatti. Nor the Haydn, Mozart, and Beethoven quartets. Not even Bach. I haven't listened to the B Minor Mass for more than a year. The idea of music has seemed totally foreign to me for some time now. I can't think any more why anyone would want to bother with sounds in that way. I can stand on the platform in the Underground and listen to the wincing of the rails as the train comes in, listen to the rumble as it goes. I can listen abstractly to the football players on the common, trains going by, aeroplanes overhead. Raw sound I don't mind but music has nothing to do with me any more. And it's not as if I can meditate or anything like that. It's just that plain sounds and silence are all I want to hear.

On my Friday half-day I went to the Zoo again. One of the keepers in the Aquarium came out of a PRIVATE door and I asked him about the turtles. The big ones have been there twenty or thirty years, he said. I asked him if it was possible to look at the tank from the other side. Yes, he said, and took me into PRIVATE.

One had to go up a few steps and climb through a hole in the wall, then there were planks across the back of the tank. It was brightly lit, had a backstage feeling. The turtles looked different seen from above.

'That's not the colour they'd be in natural light,' the keeper said. 'Their colour fades here.'

'Would it be a big job moving them out of here?' I said.

'We do it sometimes when we clean the tank,' he said. 'Put them in the filters. Bit awkward getting them through the hole, you have to mind their jaws. But it's not too difficult.'

'Suppose,' I said, 'some sort of turtle freak decided to steal the turtles and put them back in the ocean. What would he need for the job?'

'You're talking about me,' he said. 'That's what I've wanted to do. I've told them we ought to let the big ones go, replace them with little ones. We go fishing off Southampton for specimens two or three times a year, and I've said why don't we take the big turtles along and put them into the Channel. Apart from wanting them to go free I'm tired of cleaning up after them. But they don't want to know, they're not interested in the turtles here.'

'Wouldn't transport be a problem?' I said. 'Don't

they have to be kept from drying out? And isn't the Channel too cold for them?'

'Funny,' he said. 'You're the second this week that's asked me about turtle transport. A lady was chatting to me about the turtles the other day. Sometimes no one asks about them for six months at a stretch. Drying out's no problem on a trip as short as from here to Southampton. Put them on wet sacks, they'd even be all right without anything for that distance. I don't think the water'd bother them. Cold water makes them a little sluggish but I think they'd backtrack up the North Atlantic Current till they hit the Canary Current or the Gulf Stream. I bet they'd be in home waters in three months.'

'The lady,' I said, 'was she rather arty-intellectual looking? Husky voice?'

'That's the one,' he said. 'Friend of yours?'

'No,' I said. 'Then there isn't all that much to it, is there? Just a matter of hiring a van and taking along a trolley or something. But the place must be guarded at night?' I wondered when he'd start looking at me hard and ask me about the questions I was asking.

'Securicor,' he said. 'But they make their rounds on a regular schedule. That's no problem.'

Was he inviting me to have a go at it? I liked the look of him, he seemed a right sort of man. Suddenly it all seemed hugely possible, I began to go trembly. 'It's been nice talking to you,' I said, and got his name and telephone number. George Fairbairn. He's the Head Keeper. It seemed almost too much to think about at the moment, almost as if it were thrusting itself upon me. And what had *she* in mind for the turtles? Probably the same sort of lark or at least the same sort of fantasy. Funny, two minds full of turtle thoughts.

I 2

Neaera H.

Children in the sunlight and the green shade of the square. They seem shaped of light, of silver air or green shade, changing substance as they move from one to the other. Their little shouts and cries are like coloured dots that make a picture of noise but looked at closely the dots are coloured silence. High-legged and quick the children wade in twos and threes through light and shade like shore birds.

What I do is not as good as what an oyster-catcher does. Writing and illustrating books for children is not as good as walking orange-eyed, orange-billed in the distance on the river, on the beaches of the ocean, finding shellfish. And of course they fly as well which must be worth a good deal. Oyster-catchers fit into the world, their time fits. I don't know how long they live. Herring gulls can live as long as twenty-eight years. The eyes of herring gulls are utterly pitiless, have no pity even for the bird they're part of. They seem not to be bird eyes but ocean eyes, yellow eyes of the ocean looking out of the bodies of birds.

The man in the bookshop who knew about Carr, his eyes too seemed other than of himself, seemed not to be seeing things on his behalf. It was as if he found himself always in strange houses looking out of the windows of rooms in which nothing was his. A tall hopeless-looking man with an attentive face and an air of fragile precision like a folding rule made of ivory. There was something in my memory: *The Man in the Zoo*, the David Garnett novella about the man who had himself locked up in a cage and exhibited as *Homo sapiens*. Not that he seems part of such a story but the idea of him has something of hapless patience in it.

George Fairbairn, the Head Keeper at the Aquarium, seemed quite willing to tell me anything I wanted to know about the turtles. I have the feeling that if I told him what's in my mind he might even help me do it and of course that frightens me.

I can't possibly do it alone. I'd need someone to handle the turtles and drive the van, I can't do any part of it really except pay the expenses. There'd be the long drive to Cornwall, it would be night-time. I'd put them into the ocean at Polperro. The mystery of the turtles and their secret navigation is a magical reality, juice of life in a world gone dry. When I think of the turtles going into the ocean I think of it happening in that place that so badly needs new reality.

The ends of things are always present in their beginnings. T. S. Eliot has of course noted that. But it seems to me that the ends are actually *visible* in the faces of the people with whom one begins something. There is always an early face that will be forgotten and will be seen again. Sometimes one simply sees the death that will come too soon, as I did with Geoffrey long before the afternoon with the kestrel. But there's something else, some aspect of the person that is always seen early and will inevitably be seen again no matter how the seeing changes in between. The man who looks a rotter at first and then is seen to be charming will look a rotter again, that can be depended on. The scared person will look scared again, the lost one lost. That man at the bookshop has been seen as hopeless-looking long ago by someone, by himself as well, and his face has returned to that look. My face does not look back at me now when I look into the mirror. That too is a return.

More and more I'm aware that the permutations are not unlimited. Only a certain number of things can happen and whatever can happen *will* happen. The differences in scale and costume do not alter the event. Oedipus went to Thebes, Peter Rabbit into Mr McGregor's garden, but the story is essentially the same: life points only towards the terror. Beatrix Potter left it to John Gould to show us Peter dangling from the beak of *Bubo bubo*.

The turtle in Lear's *Yonghy-Bonghy-Bò* looks like a hawksbill in the drawing. The man at the bookshop has not got a tiny body nor does his head grow too large but there is a good deal of Yonghy-Bonghy-Bò in him.

> Through the silent-roaring ocean
> Did the turtle swiftly go;
> Holding fast upon his shell
> Rode the Yonghy-Bonghy-Bò.
> With a sad primeval motion
> Towards the sunset isles of Boshen ...

Madame Beetle is shaped somewhat like a sea turtle, especially in profile. Seen from above she's more elongated, less shield-shaped. Her motion is primeval but not sad. Today I cleaned the tank and the filter and she's been patrolling her domain with renewed interest, repeatedly going up and down one side that was green with algae and is now clear. I wonder if she's looking at her reflection. 'Domain,' I said as if she were free and not the prisoner of my flagging invention. The shipwreck looks quite good now, a little furry and spotty, its foretop lost in green curling fronds. All of the plants are putting out new growth.

Very naval Madame Beetle looks, as neat and boaty as a model at the Science Museum. Her underside is tan with regular transverse black lines as neat as the planking one sees in models. A Victorian one-man submarine perhaps, or a little armoured galley. Up and down the sides she goes then once round the tank rowing her smooth and undulating course. Beyond her little ocean I see rooftops and the sky.

I was on the South Bank one day by the Royal Festival Hall. It was a sunny day with a bright blue sky. I was looking up at a train crossing the Hungerford Bridge. Through the train I could see the sky successively framed by each window as the carriages passed. Each window moving quickly forward and away held briefly a rectangle of blue. The windows passing, the blue remained.

13

William G.

Now suddenly the weather is hot, the days are heavy and humid. There are more and more strong-voiced people in the shop with sunglasses and cameras and American Express Travellers' Cheques. Many American couples as they age seem to make a sexual exchange: the man looks feminine, the woman masculine. Or perhaps the woman takes over both sexes and the man vacates his altogether. One big strong leathery lady was in yesterday buying guidebooks and maps. She seemed to be carrying her husband under her arm as some ladies carry little dogs on buses. 'You'd better go buy some antiques, John,' she said to him. 'I'm going to be here for a while.' 'Right,' said John when she'd set him on his feet. He went out with his telephoto lens thrusting before him like a three-foot optical erection. If the authorities ever twig what cameras are about they'll make old men stop flashing their telephotos.

The ocean is striking back. In this morning's *Times* there was an item about a Japanese seaweed called *Sargassum muticum* that's spreading everywhere. It fouls propellers and traps boats, said the report. That was to be expected.

Saturday afternoon I went to the Zoo again. The sunlight was brilliant in Regent's Park, the air was sticky with ice-cream and soft drinks, people were rowing boats, there were girls in bikinis everywhere in the green grass and young men walking with their shirts off. Inside the Aquarium it seemed darker than ever. I scarcely looked at the turtles, saw them out of the corner of my eye swooping like bad dreams in the golden-green.

I found George Fairbairn and we went into the room behind the turtle tank. There was another room off that one with a lot of small tanks in it, and he showed me a little turtle somebody'd given the Aquarium when they found out how big it would grow. It was some kind of Ridley he thought but he wasn't sure which kind. I held it in my hand. One wouldn't expect a little black sea turtle to be cuddly but it was. It was about nine inches long, heavy and solid, and waggled its flippers in a very docile way. It felt such a iolly nice little piece of life.

After we'd been chatting for a while I came right out with it, standing there between two rows of tanks with the little turtle in my hand. There were big cockroaches hopping about on the floor. 'What if the turtle freak were to propose a turtle theft to the Head Keeper?' I said.

'Head Keeper wouldn't be all that shocked by it,' he said.

'How would we go about it?' I said.

'Best time would be when we're cleaning and painting the tank,' he said. 'We take the turtles out and put them in the filters and they stay there for a week maybe while the maintaining gets done. So they're not on view and maybe for the whole week the Society wouldn't even know they're gone.'

'But if you help me do it there's really no way of hiding your part in it, is there?' I said.

59

'No,' he said, 'I guess there isn't.'

'Would they bring charges against you?' I said. 'Would you get sacked?'

'They wouldn't bring charges,' he said, 'and I don't think I'd be sacked either. I'm Head Keeper and I've been here twenty-seven years, that counts for something. They'd take it up at a Council meeting and consider my reasons but they'd be batting on a sticky wicket actually. The R.S.P.C.A.'s always interested in anything that might be considered cruelty to animals and if I said that keeping the turtles here was cruel the Zoological Society mightn't want to push it too far.'

What about me? I wondered. Would I be had up for it? Not unless George Fairbairn grassed on me, and he wasn't the sort to do that. 'Are you willing to do it?' I said.

'Yes,' he said. 'It's one of those things that's pretty well got to be done. I'll let you know a couple of days in advance when we're going to clean the tank. It won't be for a month or two yet. Where're you thinking of launching them?'

'Brighton?' I said. Brighton was close, and I was beginning to want it over and done with as quickly as possible.

'Brighton's as good as any place I suppose. Although they might have a better chance starting out farther west.'

'Where'd they come from?' I said.

'Madeira.'

Madeira. The name sounded like boats and sunlight. I gave him my telephone numbers at the shop and at home. We shook hands and I left without looking at the turtles. They'd become an obligation now, and heavy.

On my way to the South Gate I saw the woman who'd been in the shop asking about turtle books. She was coming towards me, heading for the Aquarium I had no doubt. Damn you, I thought, surprised at the violence of my feelings. Damn her for what? I might as well damn myself as well, for not being young, for being middle-aged and nowhere and unhappy, for having turtle fantasies instead of living life. She had turtle business in mind, I was certain of it. And I knew she was going to ask me some kind of direct question and I was going to answer it and then we'd both be in it, it wouldn't be just mine any more. It was the sort of situation that would be ever so charming and warmly human in a film with Peter Ustinov and Maggie Smith but that sort of film is only charming because they leave out so many details, and real life is all the details they leave out.

She was looking at me and I couldn't look away or pretend not to recognize her. Damn her, damn her I thought. We both stopped and I could see her turning the whole thing over in her mind. She has the kind of face that doesn't hide anything, you can read it right off. Vulnerable, I suppose. Why hasn't she learned not to be vulnerable, she's old enough. She was certainly going to speak, was bound to speak, couldn't help but speak but it was difficult for her, she felt shy. Suddenly I felt sorry for her. Maybe she'd been thinking about the turtles longer than I had, maybe I and not she was the one who was intruding. All right, I thought, I'm sorry. Go ahead, speak.

'Hello,' she said, and went on past me.

'Hello,' I said.

Why didn't she speak?

14

Neaera H.

> Alas! What boots it with uncessant care
> To tend the homely slighted Shepherds trade,
> And strictly meditate the thankles Muse,
> Were it not better don as others use
> To sport with Amaryllis in the shade,
> Or with the tangles of Neaera's hair?

Fathers are prone to name first daughters elaborately.
I don't mind so much being named after a nymph but
I really don't care to be associated with the pastoral
tradition. An idyll based on illusion has no charm for
me, but then of course idylls are almost by definition
illusion. Even the lovely music of *Acis and Galataea*
does not incline me favourably towards nymphs and
swains. I think a shepherd ought to tend sheep and a
poet ought to write poems. If I owned sheep I don't
think I'd send them out with a poetic shepherd. Although if one forgets the shepherds of Theocritus and
thinks of David herding sheep while armed with a
sling that's quite different. David, yes indeed. A poet-
shepherd with a strong right arm. I wonder why I
never thought of him in that light before.

My hair is often tangled and no one withes it now.
There are fashions in emotion as in other things. If I
were twenty now and my fiancé died in a car crash I
think I should soon find another man. My generation
was somewhat in between things, neither free nor much
supported by whatever held us in. More of us were
capable of being brought to a halt by something of

that sort than young people now would be. Our songs were different, our dances and our choices. Rubbish. Even in the privacy of my own mind I can't be entirely honest with myself.

The man from the bookshop, when I saw him at the Zoo I thought he was going to say something to me. I had the feeling that he was coming from the Aquarium, that he had turtles on his mind. All he said was 'Hello,' and we went our separate ways. It's curious how the mind works. I see the world through turtle-coloured glasses now. Because of the turtles I expect a stranger to speak significantly, am prepared for signs and wonders, my terrors freshen, I feel a gathering-up in me as if I'm going to die soon, I await a Day of Judgment. Whose judgment? Mine, less merciful than God's. It is not always a comfort to find a like-minded person, another fraction of being who shares one's incompleteness. The bookshop man has many thoughts and feelings that I have, I sense that.

I went into the Aquarium but I didn't see George Fairbairn and I was glad not to have the chance to talk further about the turtles. The Aquarium was intensely dark after the violent sunlight outside, I could scarcely see the benches down the middle of it. Young couples were black against the green-lit windows of the tanks. I sat on the bench nearest the turtles but I didn't look directly at them. At one particular moment that part of the Aquarium was empty except for the turtles and the fish and me. Then a young man and a girl came out of the darkness and stood in front of the turtles. He murmured something that I couldn't quite make out, and she said in a voice that was like a clear mirror, 'No, it's too late, it's too late.'

I was surprised at the effect of her words on me. I

didn't burst into tears. I didn't know what she was re-
ferring to — it might have been love or theatre tickets
but it struck me at once that her observation was
probably accurate. Very likely it *was* too late for whatever they were talking about. She sounded the sort of
girl who sees things clearly, and young as she was there
was something for which it was too late.

Too-lateness, I realized, has nothing to do with age.
It's a relation of self to the moment. Too-lateness is
potentially every moment. Or not, depending on the
person and the moment. Perhaps there even comes a
time when it's no longer too late for anything. Perhaps,
even, most times are too early for most things, and most
of life has to go by before it's time for almost anything
and too late for almost nothing. Nothing to lose, the
present moment to gain, the integration with long-
delayed Now. Headlights staring out on sleeping
streets. Sea-smelling turtles and the smell of wet
hessian from the sacking. The tide in or out drawn by a
moon seen or unseen.

The man from the bookshop, would he be willing to
drive the van? I think he's perhaps already thought of
it, without me of course. Possibly it isn't something
he'd like to share with anyone, I might be intruding.
But the turtles are after all public, so to speak. Perhaps
they no longer want the ocean and I'm wrong to im-
pose my feelings on them. But I believe they do want
the ocean, that must be in them. No, it's not always a
comfort to find a like-minded person. If the bookshop
man and I both have designs on the turtles we have got
to muddle through it as decently as possible but there's
little to be said between us beyond that. We've too
much in common for us to be comfortable in each
other's presence for very long.

15

William G.

They won't stop killing the whales. They make dog-
and cat-food out of them, face creams, lipstick. They
kill the whales to feed the dogs so the dogs can shit on
the pavement and the people can walk in it. A kind of
natural cycle. Whales can navigate, echo-locate, sing,
talk to one another but they can't get away from the
harpoon guns. The International Whaling Com-
mission is meeting here in London right now but they
won't stop the killing of whales.

The drinking fountain on the common is gone. It
was there for years and years, probably ever since the
footpaths and the playground and the paddling pool
and the football pitch were made. The people next
door have been here for twenty years and it was there
when they moved in. Vandals pushed it over the other
night, broke the pipes. Now it's been taken away.
There's a little square hole full of water with a Coca-
Cola tin in it and that's all.

There's something about the common at night,
something about the dark open space facing the lighted
houses that provokes savagery and terrorism. Youths
on the common at night yell horribly as they pass the
houses. They feel themselves to be part of the night
outside and they want the people inside to be afraid.
They get into the playground and scream and shout
and hurl the swings about with a savage clashing of

the chains as if they could destroy the world by pulling down the playground. In the morning the chains are all wound round the crossbar and the maintenance man has to come with a ladder to disentangle the swings.

The drinking fountain and the whales are all part of the same thing in my mind. I feel as if the life is being torn out of the world.

Fear. Some days I have to go to the loo three times before I leave the house in the morning. I can feel the fear thrilling in me the same way the rails feel the trains coming. Fear of everything. I wasn't sorry to give Dora the car when we parted, I hated to drive it, always felt as if something dreadful might happen at any moment. I never felt as manly and powerful as other male drivers. When I stopped at traffic lights I never pulled up nose to nose with other cars, always stopped a little way back so as not to challenge anyone. If I take the turtles to Brighton I'll have to drive the van but that'll be all right. The turtles are depending on me. *Something*'s depending on me.

I was looking at a book on shamanism at the shop, by Mircea Eliade. In Siberia and South America, wherever they have shamans, they're always the unstable, the epileptics, the weird ones of the group, people prone to terrors and depression as I am. But unlike me they get initiated into power and a place of importance, they become seers and healers. There's something between them and animals, a bond, a connection, channels of power. Speech with animals, magical transformations. Could I be a turtle. Could I through an act of ecstasy swim unafraid and never lost, finding, finding? Swimming with Pangaea printed on my brain and bones, the ancient continent that was before the land masses drifted apart. That's part of it

66

too: there were no seas between, the land was one, there was one thing, unbroken. Now there are thousands of miles of open water and the strong ones, the swimmers, the unlost, are driven to trace the paths between, maintain the ancient connection. I don't know whether I can keep going. A turtle doesn't have to decide every morning whether to keep on bothering, it just carries on. Maybe that's why man kills everything: envy.

A confusion of fixed and flashing lights confronts the navigator, that's what the sign on the Port Liberty model says. That's how life seems to me sometimes. At other times it's a confusion of fixed and flashing darknesses. More darknesses than lights I think. Port Liberty doesn't exist and Pangaea having separated will never again come together. Unless he is already doomed, Fortune favours the man who keeps his nerve. *Beowulf.* Of course it's easy to keep your nerve when you've got a grip that can tear the arm right off a sea monster. Am I doomed? Flashing darkness is pretty much the same as flashing light really. Fear isn't at all the same as courage but after a certain point perhaps being afraid of everything is the same as being afraid of nothing. It doesn't feel that way now but then I haven't reached that point yet. If the fool would persist in his folly he would become wise, said Blake. If the coward persists in his cowardice does he become brave?

Maybe I could stop smoking, that would give me more years to get brave in. It's getting to my legs, they seize up on me now whenever I climb stairs. When I stopped smoking for nine days not long ago I could run right up the stairs in the Underground like other people.

I've met several other men who were divorced and

didn't see their children any more because their wives had left the country. It didn't seem to bother them all that much. I feel as if it'll kill me but then when I was with the children I felt that being married to Dora was taking my life away. Maybe I'm just one of those people so accustomed to being miserable that they use the material of any situation to fuel their misery.

Sometimes I think it must help to have a conviction in one's birthplace, to feel a significance in having been born in one place rather than another. Perhaps if more of my childhood had been spent in Polperro I'd feel stronger about it. My father retired there to paint, met my mother in the teashop where she worked, married her and died two years later. I was one year old when Mother and I came to London and I still can't see the point of my having been born in Polperro. I've never been back there.

For some time now on bad days I've been falling back on a news item I read last month. An important witness in the current American government scandal was said to be desperately afraid of going to prison because he's so good-looking that all the homosexuals will be after him. I have many problems but not that one.

16

Neaera H.

The one beach pebble I have from my childhood is the one I call my Caister two-stone. It's an amalgam of two different kinds of material, half grey and half brown.

My father took me to the Caister Lifeboat Station once. There was no boathouse like the one that's there now, the boat, the *Charles Burton*, was on skeets on the sand. It had saved seven lives that year. One of the vessels the Caister men had helped was the *Corn Rig* of Buckie. 'Rendered assistance' was the expression used. 'We rendered assistance to the *Corn Rig* of Buckie,' said the brown-faced man my father was talking to. It had a gallant sound like a line in a narrative poem. My father said to me afterwards that Caister men never turn back. 'They may die, they may drown, but they never turn back,' he said wonderingly and shook his head. His words and the words of the other man have stayed together in my mind:

> We rendered assistance to the *Corn Rig* of Buckie,
> We may die, we may drown, but we never turn back.

As if to reprove the Caister men for their obstinate courage the Royal National Lifeboat Institution took away their boat and shut down the station several years ago, economizing the service. The Caister men of course got themselves another boat and carry on unofficially. The stone is on my desk and I handle it often.

This preoccupation with the turtles, this project that insists on forming itself in my mind, wants to be seen in its proper light. I have got to try to understand it a little better. Not perhaps entirely, I'm not given to examining too closely the actions that really matter. I can deliberate long over a dinner-party invitation, considering carefully every aspect of the occasion and what it will cost me in time and equilibrium but when the venture is crucial I simply trust to luck and plunge into the dark. And even now at the age of forty-three I still can't say whether I've been lucky or unlucky. Sometimes it looks one way and sometimes the other.

On reflection I really don't want to understand it better. It may be silly and wrong and useless, it may be anything at all but it seems to be a thing that I have to do before I can do whatever comes after it. That it seems to involve other people is inevitable, everything does in one way or another.

I went to the bookshop. The man and I said hello to each other and I went to the Natural History section where I turned the pages of books without looking at them. My heart was pounding somewhat and I found myself mentally rehearsing what I would say. I always do that, I can't help it. Even when I go to the Post Office I say in my mind before I reach the window, 'Twenty stamps at 3p, please.' Then I say it aloud at the window. 'I wonder if you too are thinking about the turtles?' I would say. Or 'Perhaps we had better discuss the turtles?' I cursed him for not being man enough to speak up and broach the subject when it loomed so large and visible between us.

I became aware that he was standing near me emanating silence and in my mind I cursed him again.

'The turtles ...' I blurted out.

'The turtles ...' he mumbled at the same time. We both laughed.

'It's almost lunch-time,' he said. 'Perhaps we could talk about it then. Can you wait a few minutes?'

I nodded and went to the Poetry section, opened A. E. Housman at random and read:

> The world is round, so travellers tell,
>   And straight though reach the track,
> Trudge on, trudge on, 'twill all be well,
>   The way will guide one back.
>
> But ere the circle homeward hies
>   Far, far must it remove:
> White in the moon the long road lies
>   That leads me from my love.

It was James Haylett of Caister who first said that Caister men never turn back. He was a lifeboatman for fifty-nine years, and at the age of seventy-eight he went into the surf and pulled out his son-in-law and one of his grandsons from under the lifeboat *Beauchamp* the night it capsized in November, 1901. At the inquiry it was suggested that the *Beauchamp*, which had gone to the rescue of a Lowestoft fishing-smack on the Barber Sands, might have turned back because of the force of the gale and the heavy seas. That was when James Haylett said, 'Caister men never turn back.' Nine of the lifeboat crew were lost including two sons and a grandson of James Haylett. The fishing-smack had got herself off the sands, anchored safely in deep water, and knew nothing of the disaster until later. Rescuers and those to be rescued don't always come back together.

Lunch-time came. We went to a little place near by

where the take-away queue waited partly in the street
and partly at the counter. There were no empty booths
so we shared one with two fresh-faced young executives
eating eggs and sausages and grease.

'The brief is really quite clear,' said the one next to
me.

'We've put in the think time,' said the one next to the
bookshop man. 'We're ready to move on it.'

'And we'd jolly well better do it soon,' said mine.
'Those chaps in the City can't be kept dangling in-
definitely. Once we've separated the sheep from the
goats we've got to make our bid.'

'Precisely what I said in my report,' said the other
as he wiped up some grease with a bit of Mother's
Pride sliced bread. 'When they get back from Stuttgart
I want to see some action.'

Their faces were pink, their eyes were clear and
bright, their shirts and ties what the adverts call co-
ordinated I believe. Mine had dirty fingernails and his
handkerchief was tucked into his jacket sleeve. The
other had clean fingernails. Their voices were loud,
they were eager to impart the dash and colour of their
lives to the drabness about them.

I had a salad. If I were to say that today's tomatoes
are an index of the decline of Western man I should be
thought a crank but nations do not, I think, ascend on
such tomatoes. The bookshop man had fried eggs with
sausages, chips, grease and Mother's Pride sliced
bread and butter. He put ketchup on the chips. No
wonder he looks hopeless I thought.

'I always bring a sandwich for lunch,' he said. 'But I
can have it for tea.'

'If the bananas aren't unloaded soon they'll spoil,' I
said. I felt like talking like a spy.

'I'm waiting to hear from our friend at the docks,' said the bookshop man, rising in my estimation. 'I can't arrange the haulage until he gives me a date.'

The two young executives raised their eyebrows at each other.

'Have you booked them right the way through?' I said. The waitress reached across us with sweets for the executives. Mine had trifle, the other fruit salad with cream.

'Only tentatively,' said the bookshop man. 'Brighton's close.'

'I was thinking of Polperro,' I said.

The bookshop man went very red in the face. 'Polperro!' he said. 'Why in God's name Polperro?'

I indicated the two executives with my eyes and busied myself with my salad. They were both having white coffee with a lot of sugar. Life mayn't always be that sweet for you I thought.

There was a long silence during which the executives smoked a kingsize filter-tip cigarette and a little thin cheap cigar without asking me if I minded. The bookshop man took something from his pocket and began to play with it. It was a round beach pebble, a grey one.

'Where's it from?' I said.

'Antibes,' he said. 'I haven't smoked all morning.'

The executives excused themselves. We had coffee, no sweets. On the wall two booths away from us was a circular blue fluorescent tube in a rectangular wire cage. It was probably some kind of air purifier but it looked like a Tantric moon or some other contemplation object. I contemplated it. The bookshop man looked into his coffee as if viewing the abyss.

'Did I say anything wrong?' I said. 'About Polperro?'

'No,' he said. 'It just took me by surprise. Why Polperro?'

'If I said that Polperro and the turtles together add up to something, would that mean anything to you?' I said.

He looked at me strangely. 'Yes,' he said.

On the way out I went over to the Tantric moon and read the nameplate on it. INSECT-O-CUTOR, it said.

'I'll ring you up when I hear from George Fairbairn,' said the bookshop man.

I gave him my name and telephone number.

'Neaera,' he read. 'Eldest daughter?'

I nodded.

'My name's William G.,' he said.

We shook hands and parted. Going home on the tube I was astonished at the number of paint- and ink-stains on the skirt I was wearing.

William G.

Neaera H. The penny didn't drop until a few minutes after we'd parted, then I remembered the Gillian Vole books, Delia Swallow, Geoffrey Mouse and all the others I used to read to the girls. *Delia Swallow's Housewarming* was Cyndie's favourite for a long time, she never tired of it. This must be the same Neaera H., she looked too much like a writer-illustrator not to be one.

Back at the shop I went to Picture Books in the Juvenile section and looked at a copy of *Delia Swallow's Housewarming*. No photograph or biographical details on the back flap. All it said was that Delia Swallow, though the stories were written for children, had long been a favourite with readers of all ages, as had Gillian Vole etc. I looked at the first page:

> 'Just any eaves won't do,' said Delia Swallow to her husband John when they were looking for a nest.
> 'I'd like eaves on the sunny side and with a view.'
> 'Field or forest?' said John.
> 'Field with forest at the edge I think,' said Delia.
> 'Riverside or hill?' said John.
> 'Riverside with a hill behind,' said Delia.
> 'Right,' said John, and went to sleep.
> He always kipped after lunch.

Ariadne and Cyndie always liked it that John Swallow kipped after lunch. In the evenings he usually dropped in for a pint or two and a game of darts at the *Birds of a Feather*, after which:

He sometimes flew a little wobbly going home.

Strange. While I was married to Dora and living in Hampstead and working at the agency Neaera H. was writing those books. Now here we are, both of us alone and thinking turtle thoughts. At least I assume she's alone. She looks as if she's always been alone. Of course I'm seeing her out of alone eyes, I could well be wrong.

The turtles share a tank at the Zoo. I share a bath at Mrs Inchcliff's. Hairy Mr Sandor. I taped a little sign to the bathroom wall:

PLEASE CLEAN BATH AFTER USING

Not that it'll do much good. It's not too bad really, he only baths a couple of times a week. Miss Neap baths daily and when she's been before me the bathroom smells very blonde and militantly fragrant, as if mortality could be kept at bay by lavender in the same way that garlic repels vampires. If Dracula and Miss Neap were to have a go I think he'd be the one to come away with teeth marks in his throat.

When I had a bathroom of my own. I think about that sometimes. When I was an account executive. When I owned a house. When my daughters sat on my lap and I read to them. When they collected pebbles with me on the beach. Ariadne's twenty now, Cyndie's eighteen. I haven't seen them for three years. I don't know where they are.

The past isn't connected to the future any more. When I lived with Dora and the girls the time I lived in, the time of me was still the same piece of time that had unrolled like a forward road under my feet from the day of my birth. That road and all the scenes along it belonged to me, my mind moved freely up and down it. Walking on it I was still connected to my youth and strength, the time of me was of one piece with that time. Not now. I can't walk on my own time past. It doesn't belong to me any more.

There's no road here. Every step away from Dora and the girls leads only to old age and death whatever I do. No one I sleep with now has known me young with long long time and all the world before me. Rubbish. I remember how it was lying beside Dora in the night. O God, I used to think, this is it and this is all there is and nothing up ahead but death. The girls will grow up and move out and we'll be left alone together. I remember that very well. It's the thisness and this-onlyness of it all that drives middle-aged men crazy.

Why turtles for God's sake? Helping them find what they're looking for won't bloody help me. And now I'm lumbered with it. I'll have to find out what it costs to hire a van. I wonder if the two of us can get the turtles on to the trolley. She doesn't look that strong. We'll need a board or something for a ramp. Maybe I should build crates for them, they'd be easier to handle that way. I hate details. And now it's got to be Polperro just to make life more difficult. I know there'll be some kind of physical problem like having to climb a million steps or lower ourselves by ropes or the tide will be out and we'll have to drag the turtles across a mile of mud in the dark. What on earth can Polperro mean to her?

I saw a film years ago, *The Swimmer*, with Burt Lancaster. In it he was an American advertising man whose mind had slipped out of the present. He thought he still had a wife and children and a house but it was all gone. The film began with a golden late-summer afternoon. He turned up at the swimming pool of some friends who hadn't seen him for a long time. They looked at him strangely, he wasn't part of their present time any more. While he was there it occurred to him that there were so many swimming pools in that part of Connecticut that he could almost swim all the way home. So he went from pool to pool, public and private, swimming across Fairfield County meeting people from different bits of his life whilst swimming home as he thought. And wherever he went people became angry and disturbed, he didn't belong in their present time, they didn't want him in it. At the end of the film he was huddled in the doorway of the empty locked house that had been his while rain came down and he heard the ball going back and forth on the empty tennis court and the voices of his daughters who were gone. Dora and I saw the film together.

No swimming pools for me. Just a bath that I have to clean Mr Sandor's pubic hair out of while Miss Neap's lavender scent marches up and down the walls like a skeleton in armour. The water is not relaxing. Or indeed it may be relaxing, may be totally relaxed but I'm not. I don't want to be naked with anybody now, especially myself.

Haven't smoked for three days. Busy night and day not smoking. Already I can climb stairs better but that's not much of a life. With smoking one has a life while dying. How did the Greeks ever run a whole culture without it? Maybe that's why there was so much homosexuality. The turtles are no substitute for smoking. I'm tired of playing with pebbles and sucking wine gums. Breathing straight air seems an empty exercise.

I may kill somebody if I don't smoke. Mr Sandor's life is hanging by a thread if he only knew it.

Shamans in a state of ecstasy fly, travel long distances or think they do, say they do. When I was between twelve and thirteen I was lying in bed one night not asleep, not awake, and all at once I was looking down at myself from the ceiling. It wasn't a dream, I don't know what it was. I don't know anything about ecstasy. It happened another time that year too. I was standing by the window looking at myself lying in bed. Twice in my life I've been out of myself in that way. I don't think I've been into myself yet. *In* myself like a prisoner. But not into my self.

Ocean. When I think that word I want to be immersed in it and at the same time contain it all. Great green deeps of ocean. A medium of motion and being. And of course the sharks. Walking on the ground is not comparable to that underwater flying, green water touching every part.

I walk a lot at night now, sit on benches in squares feeling the dark on my face, looking at the street lamps. Most of the other people on the street are young. I don't want to sit in my room. I don't want to do anything particularly.

Actually we're all swimmers, we've all come from the ocean. Some of us are trying to find it again.

Eliade says in his book on shamanism:

In the beginning, that is, in mythical times, man lived at peace with the animals and understood their speech. It was not until after a primordial catastrophe, comparable to the 'Fall' of Biblical tradition, that man became what he is today — mortal, sexed, obliged to work to feed himself, and at enmity with the animals. While preparing for his ecstasy and during it, the shaman abolishes the present human condition and, for the time being, recovers the situation as it was in the beginning. Friendship with animals, knowledge of their language, transformation into an animal are so many signs that the shaman has re-established the 'paradisal' situation lost at the dawn of time.

That's the crux of it: abolishing the present human condition. Shamans wear bird costumes and they fly. Somehow they experience flying. They're gone and they come back with answers. Could I abolish the human condition? Could I swim, experience swimming, finding, navigating, fearlessness, unlostness? Could I come back with an answer. The unlostness itself would be the answer, I shouldn't need to come back.

18

Neaera H.

More and more I feel that I ought not to have forced myself into that man's turtle thoughts. Perhaps he wasn't even going to do anything about them, perhaps I've precipitated a harmless fantasy into an active crisis. None of us can be sufficiently sensitive. We feel our own pain wonderfully well but seldom attribute agony to others. When we were talking there were moments when his face made me think of the John Clare poem about the badger hunted out of his den by men and dogs and taken to the town and made to fight until he was dead. There's a line in which he 'cackles, groans, and dies'. William G. looked as if he might be going to cackle.

I wonder about myself. Why didn't I simply write a turtle letter to *The Times* and let it go at that? Certainly I've felt like taking some kind of action but I'm not sure I'll feel that way when the time comes. And now I've committed myself with this stranger. I have breached my own privacy as well as his and almost I wish I hadn't. How on earth are we going to get through all those hours together driving to and from Polperro? I don't think either speech or silence will be comfortable. I feel terribly uneasy about the whole thing. I haven't even considered any of the physical problems of getting the turtles into the ocean. I haven't been practical about it at all.

I'm *not* committed actually. At any rate I needn't be. For years now I've had only myself and I must be economical with that self. I can simply say that I hadn't quite understood what we were talking about when he rings me up. Or I can be up to my neck in work which is always true. I'm rather a cheerful person as long as the minutes of my days buzz at home like well-domesticated bees. When I come and go too much I'm afraid that they may fly away to swarm elsewhere. I think there still are people in Norfolk who tell the bees when the owner of the hive has died, even pin a bit of crape to the hive so the bees can mourn. When they've done their mourning they get on with making honey. One only owns the hive I suppose, never really the bees. Not like cattle.

Sometimes I think that the biggest difference between men and women is that more men need to seek out some terrible lurking thing in existence and hurl themselves upon it like Ahab with the White Whale. Women know where it lives but they can let it alone. Even in matriarchal societies I doubt that there were ever female Beowulfs. Women lie with gods and demons but they don't go looking for monsters to fight with. Ariadne gave Theseus a clew but the Minotaur was his business. There are of course many men who walk in safe paths all their lives but they often seem a little apologetic, as if they think themselves not quite honourable. And there are others, quiet men, obscure, ungifted, who yet require satisfaction of some grim thing that ultimately kills them. William G. has found some monster and ... What? Almost I think he's swallowed it. It's alive and eating inside him, much worse than if it had swallowed him.

There, I'm worrying about him. I've breached my privacy badly. There's not enough of me for that, I have no self to spare. I must keep my bees.

19

William G.

Sometimes I think that this whole thing, this whole business of a world that keeps waking itself up and bothering to go on every day, is necessary only as a manifestation of the intolerable. The intolerable is like H. G. Wells's invisible man, it has to put on clothes in order to be seen. So it dresses itself up in a world. Possibly it looks in a mirror but my imagination doesn't go that far.

It's been at least twenty-five years since I read *Crime and Punishment*. Now I'm reading it again. I'd forgotten that when Raskolnikov murdered the old lady pawnbroker, Alyona Ivanovna, he also killed her half-sister Lizaveta. Lizaveta was 'a soft gentle creature, ready to put up with anything, always willing, willing to do anything.' When she came back to the flat just after Raskolnikov had killed the old woman he had to kill her as well.

Alyona Ivanovna and Lizaveta always *do* live together, always die together. You try to kill some aspect of the intolerable and you kill the gentle and the good as well. Over and over. And whoever kills some form of the intolerable becomes himself a manifestation of it, to be killed with *his* good and gentle by someone else. Two by two up the gangway to the ark. But the waters will never recede.

I'm intolerable. It's got into me, when I feed me I feed it. There's only one way to kill it.

The idea of ringing up a van place and hiring a van and driving all those miles is so heavy I can hardly lift my head up. Bloody details. Too heavy. Too much.

❧❧ ❦❦

20

Neaera H.

It was past three in the morning and I was staring into the green murk of Madame Beetle's tank. The plants are all shrouded in long green webs of algae, there are white and ghostly bits of old meat hanging about blooming with mould, the sides of the tank are very dim. It's like the setting for a tiny horror film but Madame Beetle doesn't seem to mind. I can't think now how it could have occurred to me that I might write a story about her. Who am I to use the mystery of her that way? Her swimming is better than my writing and she doesn't expect to get paid for it. If someone were to buy me, have me shipped in a tin with air-holes, what would I be a specimen of?

I went to the bookshelves, got *The Duchess of Malfi*, sat down in my reading chair, turned to the scene where the executioners enter '*with a coffin, cords, and a bell*'. I read the Duchess's speech:

> I know death hath ten thousand several doors
> For men to take their exits; and 'tis found
> They go on such strange geometrical hinges,
> You may open them both ways ...

While I sat there looking at the lines I drifted out of wakefulness but I wasn't asleep. I was seeing Breydon Water at low tide, the oyster-catchers on the mussel beds and the water silver in the sunlight. Then it wasn't low tide any more but high water, green ocean, deep. I was in it swimming, flying, green ocean over me, under me, touching every part of me. And a glimmering white shadow coming up from below. Ah yes, my mind said, the shark's mouth too is after all a place of rest, they call them *requin*.

This is not mine, I thought, coming awake again. This is someone else's ocean, someone else's shark. I hadn't asked William G. for his telephone number when I gave him mine. I looked in the directory, not expecting to find it. He probably lived in a bedsitter and the telephone would be in someone else's name. There were seven William G.s.

It was a quarter to four. I looked at the calendar. Saturday morning. I looked at the telephone. Sometimes when I look at the telephone at that time in the morning it looks as if it just happens to be that shape at that time. I simply didn't have it in me to make possibly seven calls on the chance of finding him when I felt certain that he wasn't in the directory.

I don't know how I'd got it into my head that he lived in a bedsitter and not a flat of his own but when I thought of him at home that's where I saw him. With a very tall brown Victorian wardrobe, a sort of Palaeozoic brown upholstered chair, an indeterminate bed that metamorphosed into an indeterminate couch during the day and wallpaper that baffled the eye. Still he *might* be one of the seven William G.s in the directory. I believed it to be a matter of life or death but I couldn't make myself ring up any of the William G.s. The bookshop is open on Saturday mornings and I should have to wait until 9.30 to find out if he was there or at home.

I sat in my reading chair waiting but nothing came

to me. I am not after all a telepath or a clairvoyant. I left the flat and sat in the square resting my mind on the fountain that wasn't there. The air was heavy and still, the bronze girl would be dim in the bluish light of the street lamps, her bronze would be cool and damp, the fountain jet would be shut off, the pebbles would be glistening with dew. A police constable's footsteps approached, then the glimmer of his shirt, then the constable, one of the ones I know. They're used to seeing me about at all hours.

'Very close, isn't it,' he said.

'Yes,' I said, 'it's very close.' The constable passed on, the shirt became a glimmer again, the footsteps receded.

I could scarcely sit still. I had one of those thoughts that sometimes come in dreams and put themselves into words that stay in the mind: the backs of things are always connected to the fronts of them. This is the back of the turtle thing, I thought. What? What is it? I had a feeling of dread. The back of the turtle thing was despair. Mine? His? Not mine. My despair has long since been ground up fine and is no more than the daily salt and pepper of my life. Not mine.

The square was moving towards morning. Railings that had gleamed under the street lamps were black against the first light of day. But it was a dark dawn. Weekend weather. I went back to the flat. It was much closer inside. I felt as if I were being smothered in wet sheets. I opened all the windows. The window frames were sooty and my hands got dirty. The air outside joined the air inside, all of it was like wet sheets.

I looked down at where I had been sitting in the square. The bench was empty, the square was green and vacant in the early light like one long uninflected vowel. It seemed to have lost all particularity. The trees, the bushes, the benches had no reference to anything, were altogether incomprehensible. The fountain that wasn't there was doubly not there, was incapable of being associated with the square.

It was half-past five. I was drowsy but I didn't want to go to sleep, I didn't want to dream. I lay down and of course I did fall asleep. I dreamt that nothing had a front any more. The whole world was nothing but the back of the world, and blank. No shape to it, no colour, just utter blankness. How could even the buses have lost their shape and colour, I thought. Even from the back they're red and bus-shaped. Some part of all this blankness must be a bus. But there was no bus, no anything. Just blank terror.

Then another of those dream thoughts came to me: every action has a mother and a father and is itself the mother or the father of the action that comes out of it. An endless genealogy branching back into the past, forward into the future. There is no unattached action. I woke up and it was half-past seven.

I looked at the telephone again. Don't be ridiculous, the shape of it said. The daylight in the windows threatened rain. I had breakfast and a cigarette and then another cigarette. I walked about the flat picking things up and putting them down, shuffling through unanswered letters and unpaid bills and dire things in brown envelopes On Her Majesty's Service. In the spare room are cartons of books demoted from the active shelves. 16 Giant ARIEL, said one. OUTSPAN Lemons, said another, and in my lettering: SITTING ROOM BOTTOM. That cardboard box is twenty years old, I labelled it when we emptied the shelves at home

and packed the books to move to London. The lon-
gevity of impermanent things! I sat down in the chair
again, dozed off, woke up at a quarter to nine, left
the flat quickly and went down to the bus stop.

The bus came sooner than I expected, they always
do when I'm early. I sat next to a man with a newspaper in which I read about a 'vice girl' who'd entertained various businessmen for a pop singer. She'd
been instructed to sleep with a Mr X for a fee of £5,
said the girl. She'd been requested to dress and act
like an eleven-year-old schoolgirl and to refer fre-
quently in her conversation to certain breakfast cereals
and other products by their brand names. Mr X was
in advertising it seemed. He proved incapable, said
the girl. Incapable of sleeping, I thought, smiling at
the ambiguities of polite speech. I shouldn't be surprised if Mr X *did* have difficulty in sleeping what with
all those brand names dancing in his head.

It occurred to me then to imagine lives packaged
and labelled and ranged on shelves waiting to be
bought. I couldn't think of any likely brand names
right off except Brief Candle. And what if the in-
gredients were listed on the box? Many lives would go
unsold, they'd have to discontinue some of the range.
Sorry, we don't stock that life any more, there was no
demand for it really. Hard Slog for example or Dreary
Muddle, how many would they sell a year? On the
other hand Wealth and Fame would move briskly even
with a Government Health Warning on the packet.

It was only five past nine when I got to the bookshop,
and I spent the next twenty minutes looking at the
books in the window. I observed that Taura Strong
continues to be productive, ecology was enjoying a
rising market, sex was holding its own but a little

more quietly than formerly: there were glossy books with photographs of naked people kneading each other thoughtfully. Gangsterism in government was under examination in America and government in gangsterism was being looked at as well. The backs of things are getting into print more and more these days and heterosexuality is increasingly thin on the ground in biographies. Fallopia Bothways, smiling a virile smile on the showcard for her new novel, has changed her haircut. Through the glass doors I could see the books on tables and shelves resting quietly and holding themselves in reserve until opening time. I found myself mentally turning away from the too-muchness of them.

At 9.25 a girl who seemed to have bought Hard Slog arrived with keys and unlocked one of the glass doors top and bottom. She smiled briefly, went in and locked the door behind her. I waited while she picked up the morning post, turned on the lights, went to the office at the rear of the shop, came back with brown paper bags and put money into the till. Then she looked up, seemed gratified by my patience, smiled and opened the door.

'Good morning,' I said.

'Good morning,' she said. 'Can help you?'

'Will Mr G. be here today?' I said.

She shook her head. 'It's his Saturday off.'

'Can you tell me where to reach him, his phone number?' I said. 'It's rather urgent.'

She looked at me carefully. Did I look like an old girl friend who rings up and breathes into the telephone, I wondered. I didn't think so. She shook her head with some reluctance I thought but still she shook it.

'Our manager, Mr Meager, is quite firm about that,'

she said. 'Best thing is to come in again on Monday, Mr G.'ll be here then.'

'I think he might not be,' I said. I watched a bus go past the door, first the front then the back. 'I think he may be quite ill. Would you mind ringing him up yourself just to make sure he's all right? I think it really is urgent.' By then I was quite possessed by my fixed idea and feeling a little demented about it.

'He looked perfectly well yesterday,' she said. 'He's probably not up yet. It's early for a Saturday off.'

I didn't say anything. I must have looked a fright.

'All right,' she said. 'I'll ring him. It's a little odd, you know. After all if you're a friend of his you'd have his number, wouldn't you.'

I couldn't think of anything to say, just looked at her dumbly.

'All right,' she said again. 'Who shall I say it is?'

'Neaera H.,' I said.

Her face changed, her manner as well. Little softenings and flutters. 'The one who does the Gillian Vole books?' she said.

'Yes,' I said.

'Well,' she said with a fleeting smile, 'I'll see if I can raise him.' She went back to the office and closed the door. Through the little office window I saw her look up the number on a list she took from a drawer. She dialled, waited, spoke while watching me through the window. I couldn't hear what she said.

'I've rung the house where he lives,' she said when she came out. 'They say he doesn't answer his door. He doesn't seem to be at home.'

'This isn't anything personal,' I said. 'It's nothing personal at all really.' I could feel my face not knowing what to do with itself.

An American lady came in. 'Have you anything on Staffordshire figures?' she said.

The girl went to the shelves, took out three books.

'I have all of those,' said the American lady. 'Is there anything else?'

'That's all there is just now,' said the girl.

'Oh, dear,' said the American lady. 'Thank you.' She left.

An intense-looking young man with long hair, a beard, an immense mackintosh and a large shoulder-bag came in and headed for the Occult section.

'Would you leave your bag at the counter, please,' said the girl. The young man flashed her a dark look, left the shoulder-bag with her, went to the shelves and appeared to be deeply interested in alchemy.

'Keep your eye on him for a moment,' said the girl. 'He pinches books.' She went back to the office, returned quickly and handed me a slip of paper with William G.'s address and telephone number on it.

'Here,' she said. 'You look as if it's important.'

'Thank you,' I said, and hurried away.

Someone got out of a taxi and I got in. Just like a film, I thought. People never have to wait for taxis in films. Old films, that is. They never used to get change when they paid for anything either, they just left notes or coins and walked away. Now they get change. Perhaps they sometimes have to wait for taxis too. I gave the driver the address, it was in S.W.6.

'Do you know the street?' he said.

'No,' I said. 'Don't you?'

'I'm a suburban driver,' he said as he turned down the Brompton Road. 'I don't know London all that well. Most of the lads graduate to London after a while, go about on a moped getting the knowledge but

I haven't bothered. I'm a Jehovah's Witness and we think God's going to step in and put things to rights in a couple of years. There won't be any taxis then.'

'What will there be?' I said looking in my *A to Z*. 'I think it's off the Fulham Road.'

'The Lord will take care of the righteous,' he said as we came to the Brompton Oratory and turned left into the Fulham Road. 'We've been interested in the year 1975 for some time.'

'You go to Fulham Broadway and turn left into Harwood Road,' I said. 'What'll you do if nothing happens in 1975?'

'A lot of people ask that question,' said the driver. 'We'll ... ' We'd come to a place where they were tearing up the street and I couldn't hear what he said.

'Sorry,' I said leaning close to the opening in the glass partition. 'I couldn't hear you.'

'We'll ... ' he said as a plane screamed low overhead.

I sank back in the seat, didn't ask again.

The house was on a crescent opposite a football pitch, a paddling pool and a playground. The far end of the crescent looked more posh, the houses a little grander and overlooking the common. William G.'s end was Georgian terraced houses, three storeys, quite plain. I paid the driver and as he drove off I wished I'd asked him about 1975 again. I really did want to know what he'd do if it came and went without the Lord's taking a stand either way. Too late, the chance was gone.

There were no nameplates, only one bell. I rang it. A fiery-looking foreign-looking man with a violent moustache answered the door. He was wearing a Middle-Eastern sort of dressing-gown that had more colour and pattern than one really cared to see in a single garment. Red velvet slippers, very white feet and ankles with very black hair. He looked as if he had strong political convictions.

'I've come to see Mr G.,' I said.

'Top,' said the man and stood aside.

I went up, stood outside William G.'s door waiting for my heart to stop pounding. Too many cigarettes. The violent-moustached man had come upstairs too and was producing violent smells in a tiny kitchen on the landing. I could ask him to force the door if necessary. I tried not to think of what we might find. I knocked.

William G. opened the door, looked startled. 'Good morning,' he said. 'Come in.'

I gasped, found nothing to say. The room was not as I had imagined it, had white walls, an orange Japanese paper lamp. Modern furniture, mail-order Danish.

'You look quite done up,' he said. 'I'll get you some coffee.'

❧❦

William G.

It was absolutely uncanny, gave me the creeps. That woman actually thought I'd been thinking of suicide.

I *had* been thinking of it right enough, I often do, always have the idea of it huddled like a sick ape in a corner of my mind. But I'd never do it. At least I don't think I'd do it, can't imagine a state of mind in which I'd do it. Well, that's not true either. I *can* imagine the state of mind, I've been in it often enough. No place for the self to sit down and catch its breath. Just being hurried, hurried out of existence. When I feel like that even such a thing as posting a letter or going to the launderette wears me out. The mind moves ahead of every action making me tired in advance of whatever I do. Even a thing as simple as changing trains in the Underground becomes terribly heavy. I think ahead to the sign on the platform at the next station, think of getting out of the train, going through the corridor, up the escalator, waiting on the platform. I think of how many trains will come before mine, think of getting on when it comes, think of the signs that will appear, think of getting out, going up the steps, out into the street. As the mind moves forward the self is pushed back, everything multiplies itself like mirrors receding laboriously to infinity, repeating endlessly even the earwax in the ears, the silence in the eyes.

When I was a child there was a mirror in the hall-way and at some point I became aware that the mirror saw more than what was simply right in front of it. It privately reflected a good deal of hallway on both sides out of the corner of its eye so to speak. By putting my nose right up against the glass I could almost see round those corners, could almost see what the mirror was keeping to itself, the whole hallway perhaps. All of it, everything, things I couldn't see. Spiders in webs in the shadows, the other side of the light through the coloured leaded glass of the door. The shadow of the postman today, tomorrow, the day after tomorrow.

My father did, I think. Commit suicide. Although they called it an accident. His car went over a cliff into the sea. On to some rocks that you can see at low tide but not high water. No collision, no skid marks or anything. My mother kept the newspaper cutting, I still have it somewhere. Who knows what might have appeared in the road coming towards him. The rest of his life maybe. At Paddington I've seen pigeons on the tube platform walk into a train and out again while the doors were still open, knowing where they didn't want to go.

Neaera H. can't be in very good shape either if her mind is running on that sort of thing. She was deathly pale when she turned up at my door. It took her a while to come out with it, then she said in a half-whisper looking down at her coffee cup that she'd had all this green water in her mind and a white shark coming up from below. Well of course they're always in me I suppose, coming up from the darkness and the deep-water chill. But I wouldn't say I'm *broadcasting* sharks, and if she's pulling them in out of the air she must be pretty well round the bend.

She told me a little about herself, and her kind of life isn't much better than mine. At least in the shop I'm out in the world, get out of myself a little. She goes for days sometimes without seeing anyone, staying up till all hours. No wonder she gets morbid. And now it seems she's on my wavelength. That's all I need. My mind isn't much of a comfort to me but at least I thought it was private. She's going to wear herself out if she keeps tuning in like that. The inside of my head is a pretty tiresome place for someone whose own head isn't all that jolly.

I must find out about a van. It's well over two hundred miles to Polperro, closer to three hundred I should think. Night driving. I'd rather drive at night than during the day but either way the thought of it fills me with dread. And I'm scared of the turtles. That big male loggerhead could take your hand off with one bite. I could ask George Fairbairn to come with us and he might do it but that's no good. Whatever this awful thing is that I've got myself into it's my thing and I've got to do it alone with that weird lady.

I can't imagine that it'll come off without some sort of disaster. If we drive all night we'll have to sleep part of the next day before starting back. I'll be away from the shop one whole day, maybe more. I can always say I'm sick. Things are pretty slow now, Mr Meager and Harriet can get along without me for a day or two. I won't say I'm sick but I won't say turtles either. I need the time off for personal reasons.

Good God, is she going to become some sort of responsibility now? Have I got to keep happy thoughts singing and dancing in my mind so as not to plunge her into a suicidal depression. How much do I know about her actually when it comes right down to it. She lives alone, writes and illustrates children's books, doesn't seem very happy. She's not interested in me romantically, I'd have felt it if she were. But we've fallen into something together whatever it might be. I don't think I want to know any more about it just now.

22

Neaera H.

Oh, dear. What have I done now? Where are my bees? Suddenly I feel a stranger in my own flat. The clutter on the drawing table, the books and papers on the desk, the typewriter, Madame Beetle in her tank and the plants in the window have all gone blank and baffling.

Caister men never turn back. But I'm not a Caister man. My Caister two-stone confers no magic, it's only a touchstone for the terrors that I try to cover up with books and papers and plants in the window. My mind feels as if it's gone into hiding from me and is reflecting privately on matters of its own. Identity is a shaky thing. This is my place, my work, my water-beetle. Silly. Water-beetles can't be owned any more than bees can. Nothing can be owned for that matter. A typewriter? Not really. You pay for the machine, keep it in your flat, use it. But I might go out one day and never come back and the typewriter would remain, belonging only to itself. When a ewe licks a new-born lamb all over I believe that's called owning it but the ewe never really owns the lamb. That awful gathering-up feeling is in me again. My life can't be drawing to a close yet. I'm not greedy but it can't be ending so soon. Who will tell my bees and will they make honey for their next mistress. Same bees, different people, over and over.

If I could see an oyster-catcher ... No, it isn't just the bird, it's the distance, the wideness. I am so *unquiet*. What have I done. Making a fool of myself is the least of it. What's happening to my mind? The green water, the white glimmer and the open jaws: my ocean and shark, not his? Mine as well as his, that certainly. I wish I'd never seen those turtles, never seen Polperro. Could someone tell the turtles, give them a bit of crape to stream behind them in the water? If it hadn't been the turtles I suppose it would have been something else.

I can't get it out of my mind, how I must have looked sitting there with the cup clattering in the saucer. 'Are you all right?' he said. 'Is anything the matter? You don't look well.'

'I'm sorry,' I said. 'You must think I'm insane, I've never done anything like this before, I had such a dreadful feeling, I thought you might be ... They gave me your address at the shop, I said it was urgent, possibly a matter of ... There was all that green water and a shark coming up from below, terrible, terrible.' I actually went on like that, blurted out all those things.

He lit a cigarette and kept shaking the match but it wouldn't go out. He blew it out. 'Why did you think I ... Why did you think it had anything to do with me?' he said, and certainly his voice was shaking.

'Well, it wasn't mine,' I said lamely, hearing how idiotic I sounded.

'How could it not be yours?' he said. He looked cruel when he said it. 'You had a dreadful feeling, a terrible dream or thought or something and you say it wasn't yours but mine. That's rather curious, isn't it?' His voice seemed to be coming from a dark and tiny place, he seemed clearer and smaller and sharper and farther away as he spoke. I felt as if I might faint.

'Stop it,' I said. 'You're not being honest.'

'Perhaps you're not either,' he said. 'Some people won't look at what's in them, they sweep everything under the carpet. Everything's quite all right with them, they're never depressed. When the shark comes up out of the dark and the chill that's somebody else's shark not theirs. *They're* all right, Jack.'

I almost hated him for that. Any situation imposes rules of some kind and a gentleman abides by them. By coming to his door in a half-crazed state I'd created a situation in which a gentleman would have been equally open even if it made him look as crazy as I was. William G. was not wholly a gentleman and I was sorry for us both.

'You're being careful,' I said.

'*I'm* being careful!' he said. 'What about you? You've had green water and a shark and now you're trying to put it on me so it won't be you that's falling apart.'

We were both frightened and angry, a long silence followed. Then we began to speak calmly and politely, avoiding the shark. We exchanged humdrums, presentable bits of ourselves: what I did, what he did, how this was and that. We became slightly acquainted in the dreariest conventional way. I wanted to be shot of the whole turtle affair and I knew he did too but there it was like a massive chain welded to leg irons on both of us and clanking maddeningly.

We couldn't get to a better place in our conversation. It simply became a matter of sitting there until we could move away from our common discomfort and go back to our separate individual ones. We repeated things that needed no repetition: I said of course we must share the cost of the van, he said he'd let me know as soon as George Fairbairn got in touch with him. We both mumbled about the possible inconvenience of having to act on short notice, both agreed that that's how it was with this sort of thing.

I went home by bus.

23

William G.

'Did Miss H. ever reach you?' Harriet said when I came into the shop on Monday.

'Yes,' I said, 'she did.'

'I hope it was all right,' she said, 'giving her your address and telephone number.'

'Perfectly all right,' I said. 'Silly of me not to have given it to her before.'

'I had no idea she was a friend of yours,' said Harriet.

'Haven't known her long actually,' I said busying myself unwrapping a shipment.

'Funny when you meet authors,' said Harriet. 'Mostly they don't look as you'd imagine them.'

'How would you have imagined her?' I said.

'Short rather than tall,' said Harriet, 'plump rather than thin. Married rather than not. She isn't married, is she?'

'No,' I said. 'She isn't.' I made a lot of noise with the wrapping paper and the conversation lapsed.

Harriet is next in line to Mr Meager and senior to me at the shop. She's about thirty and I can remember when she did her hair in the style of the Ladies-in-Waiting at the Coronation. She's a tall thin girl from quite a good family, her father is an M.P. and her face is a constant reproach even though she's not at all bad-looking. She used to dress very con-

servatively, lived at home, walked as if the streets were
full of rapists and wore shoes that looked as if they
were designed for self-defence.

I don't recall just when it happened but all of a
sudden she came in one day wearing sandals, the kind
you get at shops where they sell Arab dresses and incense. There were her white naked startled feet at the
bottom of the still conservatively dressed pleated-skirt
Harriet and I guessed she'd lost her virginity but
little else. Her nervous-looking naked feet still hadn't
left home. Thank God my feet are in shoes most of the
time. They don't look as if they will ever walk in happy
ways and I'm pleased not to see them.

Harriet's feet walked easier after a time. She took
to wearing long full skirts and cheesecloth blouses, her
hair came down. She got herself a room, stopped
wearing a bra every day and bought *Time Out* every
week.

So there was her copy of *Time Out* in the kitchen at
the shop and I had a look at the Classified adverts.
CLAIRVOYANT and HYPNOTISM were available.
ANOREXIA NERVOSA, CONSULTATIONS IN CON-
FIDENCE. Also NUDIST CLUB (Females free), MAS-
SAGE TUITION, RUBBER ENTHUSIASTS, TAROT
DIVINATION, NATURAL FOODS, CANDLE-MAKING,
ATTRACTIVE ORIENTAL CHICK (Why was she in
Miscellaneous instead of *Lonely Hearts*?), HOMOSEXUAL
MEN AND WOMEN. PICNIC—Bring just one in-
gredient to share, ENCOUNTER, GROWTH CENTRE,
QUAESITOR, KALEIDOSCOPE—Bio-Energetic Work-
shop. I glanced only briefly at *Lonely Hearts* in which
Sensitive sensual male, 23, Handsome Aquarius, 37,
and UP TO SIX DATES from only £1 offered them-
selves.

There are times when I do something and then I say: It's come to that. *That* is of course different things at different times. It's come to a lot of *thats* in my life and I suppose they'll keep happening right up to the last and final one when perhaps my last words will be: It's come to that.

BIO-FEEDBACK, said one advert. Alpha-Wave Machine. I'd read something about that in a magazine. People who can do proper meditation get into a state of quiet alertness in which their brain waves change, and there are now machines for monitoring the brain waves so you can hear yourself getting into or out of the state that produces alpha waves. I didn't think I could make even one alpha wave, I didn't think there was one quiet place in my brain. I just wished the turtles and Neaera H. would go away although sometimes I didn't. I wished that I could turn off my head, stop thinking. My dreams are usually busy with Dora and the girls so I don't even have any spare mental time when I'm asleep and I mostly wake up feeling worn out. Sexual fantasies offer a little distraction but aren't really restful. Reading is all right but not always, Dostoyevsky overstimulates my mind. Cinemas are cosy until you have to go home, TV feels like self-abuse.

Lately my fantasies have been of a place that doesn't exist. Not Port Liberty. Port Liberty is for the clear-eyed, the competent, the strong. My fantasy is of a give-up place. At County Hall maybe, in a grotty corridor, a door with frosted glass: DEPARTMENT OF CAPITULATION AND UNCONDITIONAL SURRENDER. The usual stand-up desks along the wall with dried-up biros on chains. Forms to fill in: Campaigns in which served, Terms if sought, Next of kin. A kindly Indian civil servant to give procedural advice.

One capitulates or surrenders unconditionally, signs things over and is sent to some kind of refuge for non-contenders. I never imagine the refuge, just the giving up. Whether they have TV or books or brothels I don't know but it's out of the struggle. Sleep after toil, port after stormy seas, ease after war and all that. At least there's a model of Port Liberty but the Department of Capitulation and Unconditional Surrender doesn't exist anywhere in any form. The loony-bin isn't the same thing. I'm not crazy but then maybe nobody is. So I rang up Mr Bio-Feedback.

The place was in St John's Wood. Big bright spacious flat, high ceilings. The kind of flat that so many young Americans seem to have found or inherited from expatriate uncles before rents went up and unfurnished flats became impossible to find. Mattresses on the floor with Indian spreads, many colourful cushions, some modern things, some rattan. Homemade abstractions and blown-up photos on the walls. Lots of shelves, lots of books. Expensive sound-equipment, speakers about four feet high.

The young man with the Bio-Feedback machine was a sleek and healthy beard-and-sandals American with a wonderful head of hair that looked as if it might charge him like a battery pack. Very peaceful and serene-looking, looked as if there were *mostly* alpha waves in his head. Cheques from home, I thought. Very likely never worked a day in his life. Family man too, the bathroom was full of toys and infant gear.

The alpha-wave detector was quite a modest little plastic-box affair that didn't look as if it had more than £5 worth of parts and labour in it. He'd set it up on an impressive scaffolding of planks and pipes but it still didn't look like more than £5.

'What do you do for a living?' I said.

'This,' he said peacefully. 'And I'm the company's representative for the machines so I'll be selling them too.'

I sank into one of those big plastic hassocks that look like overripe tomatoes that have hit the ground and somehow not burst.

'You?' he said while he dabbed electrolytic jelly on the side and back of my head and fitted the electrodes. I felt ashamed of my dandruff.

'Assistant in a bookshop,' I said.

'I thought it might be something literary in one way or another,' he said. He turned on the machine, set the volume. 'It's a wave frequency filter and amplifier,' he said. 'You'll hear the alpha waves.'

I listened. Dead silence.

'Close your eyes,' he said.

'I don't think I've got any alpha waves,' I said. 'I don't think I've got anything but noise and static in my head.'

'You'd be surprised,' he said. 'Everybody has alpha waves. Are you into meditation at all?'

'No,' I said. I closed my eyes. Silence from the machine. I thought of a grey heron I'd seen once flying over a marsh flapping very slowly. A nice serene thought. Silence from the machine. I let go of the heron, let myself sink back into whatever there might be to sink back into in my mind.

Cluck cluck cluck, said the machine quietly.

'That's alpha waves,' said the young man.

I drifted into it again. Cluck cluck cluck cluck, said the machine in another little burst of chicken talk.

I went on with it for a while, I'd paid £2 for the hour. Sometimes I got bursts of ten or fifteen clucks

WILLIAM G.

together and was quite pleased with myself. That
accounts for my not having gone mad, I thought.
There must be quiet places in my head where I get a
little rest now and then without knowing about it.
A cheering thought.

I took off the electrodes. 'What about *your* alpha
waves?' I said. 'Are you good at it?'

'Don't you want to keep going?' he said. 'You still
have more time.'

'I don't think I have the patience for a whole hour
of it,' I said. 'I'd like to hear you do it.'

He wired himself up with the electrodes, closed his
eyes and looked even more serene than before. Cluck
cluck cluck cluck cluck cluck, went the machine
steadily and smoothly like a Geiger counter next to a
piece of uranium. It clucked almost continuously, with
only the briefest of pauses.

I shook my head. What was there to say? He wiped
the jelly off my dandruff.

'Thank you,' I said, and got up to leave.

'Do you think you'd like to do it again?' he said.

'I don't think so,' I said. 'But it's nice to know the
alpha waves are there sometimes.'

As I was going out he said, 'I didn't give you quite a
straight answer when you asked me what I did for a
living.'

'Please,' I said, 'there's no need to, I only asked out
of curiosity.'

'Actually I've been living on money from the
States,' he said. 'But I hope to get going with this.'

I went home with my alpha waves. You never know
what you've got going for you. Who knows what other
kinds of waves are clucking along inside me, maybe
homing me in on something good somewhere, sometime.

I didn't go straight home. When I changed from the Bakerloo Line at Paddington I went up into the Main Line Station. I felt like being with a lot of people in a big open place. Ordinarily I don't like pigeons but I like them under the glass roof of Paddington Station. Mingling with the rush of people the pigeons are quite different from the way they are when plodding about in squares and being fed by people who have nothing better to feed. Intolerant of me to think that. Pigeons, turtles, what's the odds.

So much purposeful movement at Paddington, so many individual directions crossing one another, so many different lines of action! I always think that everyone else has good places to go to, they all seem so eager to get there. I sat on the low flat wooden railing by the Track One buffers and watched the figures passing in front of the light from the news-stand and under the grey glass sky of the roof. So many pretty girls! They were never so pretty when I was twenty. Two men were talking and one of them taking some change from his pocket dropped a $\frac{1}{2}$p. While looking to see what he'd dropped he kicked it without seeing it. I watched it roll along the floor to be kicked in the opposite direction by another man who didn't see it. By then the man who'd dropped it had moved on and when the $\frac{1}{2}$p stopped rolling I went over and picked it up, put it in my pocket and went home.

24

Neaera H.

In this morning's *Times* I read that the astronauts on *Skylab-2* have got two spiders with them. One of the spiders, named Arabella, has spun something like a normal web. 'Weightlessness disoriented her at the start,' says the news item from Houston, 'and her first attempts produced only a few wisps, mainly in the corners of her cage. But today, on the thirteenth day of the *Skylab-2* flight, Dr Owen Garriott was quite pleased with the work done by the spider. "This time the web is essentially, at first glance, like one you would find on the ground," Dr Garriott said.'

That Arabella should have spun any sort of web, should have made the effort at all, overwhelms me. In her place I should have sulked or been sick I am sure. She didn't even know which way was up let alone where she was or why and yet she spun a reasonably workable web out there in space. I hope they had the decency to bring along some flies for her to catch, I can't think they'd make her eat tiny frozen dinners squeezed out of tubes or whatever astronauts subsist on. And if they did bring flies those flies must appear somewhere on *Skylab-2*'s manifest: *Flies, 12 doz.* If there are flies up there no mention is made of them or how they adapted to weightlessness. Perhaps they'd use dead flies just as they use dead mice to feed the owls at the Zoo. In any case Arabella deserves a plaque on *Skylab-2*. But of course she doesn't need one, hasn't got the sort of mind that thinks about plaques. She needs no recognition, can recognize herself and spin a web wherever she may be. What good things instincts are!

Last night I had a dream thought that I held on to carefully until this morning. It was: Those who know it have forgotten every part of it, those who don't know it remember it completely. Aggravating. Those who know or don't know what? I haven't a clue and what's most annoying is that something in me knows what was meant.

There was a week of nature films on the South Bank and I went to see one about sharks. The film was made by a man of apparently unlimited wealth who fitted himself out with a large ship and any amount of special underwater gear for shark photography. He and his companions all agreed that diving among sharks was for them the ultimate challenge. They were particularly keen to encounter a great white shark, a rare species and the one most feared as a man-eater. They went from ocean to ocean looking for the great white shark and I couldn't help wondering all the time how much it was costing. I think the money spent on even one of the special diving cages would keep me in high style for half a year at least.

For a large part of the time they followed whaling ships, photographing sharks feeding on whale car-casses. Sometimes they took their pictures from inside a cage but often they swam fearlessly among the sharks. They swam among blue sharks, dusky sharks, oceanic white-tipped sharks and several other kinds but they were continually frustrated by the absence of great white sharks.

Eventually they found a great white shark which they attracted with whale oil, blood and horsemeat. It was a truly terrifying creature and they very wisely stayed in their cage while the shark took the bars in his teeth and shook it about. The wealthy man said that it had been fantastic, incredible, beyond his expectations. His friends congratulated him on the success of the expedition and the film came to an end.

I found myself resenting that man, however unreasonable it might be of me. All the money in the world does not give him the right to muck about with a direful secret creature and shame the mystery of it with words like 'fantastic' and 'incredible'. The divers were not the ultimate challenge for the shark, I'm certain of that. Socially they were out of their class, the shark would not have swum from ocean to ocean seeking *them*. It would have gone its mute and deadly way mindlessly being its awful self, innocent and murderous. It was the people who lusted for the fierce attention of the shark, like monkeys they had to make him notice them.

Money can do many things, even the great white shark can be played with by wealthy *frotteurs* in posh diving gear. But they have not really seen him or touched him because what he is to man is what is he to naked man alone-swimming. They have not found the great white shark, they have acted out some brothel fantasy with black rubber clothing and steel bars. Aluminium they were actually.

When I came out of the Queen Elizabeth Hall with the crowd there was a threadbare man playing a mouth organ. The lamps were lit along the promenade and on the bridges, trains rattled across the Hungerford Bridge, boats apparently powered by music went past with people dancing, lights glittered on the river and in the buildings across the river, there was a full moon, the night was balmy. The mouth organ buzzed its little music fiercely, the man's eyes looked out fiercely over the mouth organ. I gave him 10p, he thanked me, sent his music after me like bees.

At a party I drank more than I should have done and found myself going on and on about Oedipus and Peter Rabbit, Thebes and Mr McGregor's garden to Harry Rush of Pryntward Rush & Hope. Two days later there was a letter affirming his strong interest in my forthcoming *From Oedipus to Peter Rabbit: The Tragic Heritage in Children's Literature* and offering me a £1,000 advance on signing.

On the morning when the letter came I was thinking that possibly the biggest tragedy in children's literature is that people won't stop writing it. It was one of those mornings when there suddenly seemed nothing whatever that could be taken for granted. I felt a stranger in my own head, as if the consciousness looking out through my eyes were some monstrous changeling. Here was the implacable morning light on all the books and litter that were always there but nothing was recognizable as having significance. What in the world was it all about, I found myself wondering.

People write books for children and other people write about the books written for children but I don't think it's for the children at all. I think that all the people who worry so much about the children are really worrying about themselves, about keeping their world together and getting the children to help them do it, getting the children to agree that it is indeed a world. Each new generation of children has to be told: 'This is a world, this is what one does, one lives like this.' Maybe our constant fear is that a generation of children will come along and say: 'This is not a world, this is nothing, there's no way to live at all.'

25

William G.

Somebody'd told Harriet about a free demonstration of something called Original Therapy and she asked me if I'd like to go with her. Neither of us had any idea of what it might be and I couldn't care less but I went. Anything to keep my mind off the turtles.

The place was in Maida Vale, the people had long hair and wore sandals which they mostly took off. There were a lot of good-looking feet in the crowd. The bearded men looked like Great Men of History from the neck up: Darwin, Pasteur, Mendeleyev, Faraday. From the neck down they looked like layabouts. The girls looked better to me but then girls usually do, there seems to me to be more human solidity in women than in men. Odd how one says *girls* and men. More than half the men were boys and more than half the girls were women who looked as if they'd seen a good deal of a certain kind of life and had cooked many hundredweights of brown rice. Oriental pillows on the floor, Buddhist and Zen books on the shelves, the *I Ching*, Laing, Castaneda, Hermann Hesse, *The Whole Earth Catalog*. Smell of old incense in the air.

The Original Therapy lady was a rampant-looking woman of about forty. Shiny red hair in the style of old musical films, tight white trousers, gold sandals, silver toenails, bursting purple silk blouse. Swarthy boyfriend with a St Christopher medal and a racing-driver watch strap.

Her name was Ruby and she sounded as if she lived in a caravan, her voice and her way of talking. She began to tell us about her therapy while some of the people in the room sat in the lotus position with very straight backs and others held their heads. One girl wailed a little now and then, another muttered the whole time.

She was American, this Ruby. Told us how she'd knocked about, been a rodeo rider, done roller derbies, wrestled, had three husbands and all kinds of troubles. Discovered her Original Therapy whilst wrestling one night. Another lady had a scissors grip on her and was squeezing very hard, got a bit over-enthusiastic and wouldn't let go. Under the pressure Ruby experienced a strange alteration of consciousness.

'I was seeing all kinds of coloured lights and shooting sparks,' she said, 'and the sound of the crowd was beginning to come and go like the roar of surf far away. Something began to happen to me. I could feel myself going way way down and way way back, like thousands of years, millions of years, glaciers coming and going and the dinosaurs sinking into the swamps and the primitive trees being crushed into coal. Farther back than that even, crawling out of a warm ocean and gasping on the beach and beyond that back to the sea and smaller and smaller, all the way back to a single cell. And back beyond that to nothing, just the warm sea, what they call the primordial soup.'

Ruby went farther than the soup even, she got to a point where there was nothing, no time, no her, no anything. Then there came something like the idea of a question, a kind of original YES or NO? It put itself together as YES. There was a mystical green pattern with no sound, then a red explosion in Ruby's mind and the people in the ringside seats were picking the other lady wrestler out of their laps. That was the turning point in Ruby's life, going back to the origin of life and finding the big YES, and she was going to show us slides and then demonstrate her therapy.

A lot of the people in the room were shifting about and trying to find space on the floor to lie down. Some were smoking hash. There was one chap who looked as if he'd been thrown together by dustmen from odd bits of upholstery and discarded clothing, he asked Ruby whether when the spirit goes out of the body another spirit could come into it. He had a high choked voice, fat unshaven face.

Ruby said that nothing like that had ever happened in her experience. There were no other questions, it was quiet in the room, one or two people were asleep. The last light of the day came through the windows, smoke drifted. Then the window curtains were drawn and Ruby showed us slides.

We saw many slides of Ruby in a bikini scissors-gripping people who also wore swimsuits or shorts. 'The skin contact makes a difference,' she said. 'Smells are important too.' We saw people bursting free as they reached YES, saw their happy faces afterwards. Ruby told us that people were revitalized in a variety of ways by returning to the origins of life via her scissors-grip. Illnesses disappeared and one man who'd been losing his hair stopped losing it.

The curtains were pulled back. It was evening now, the dim light of the street lamps came a little way into the room, ended in darkness. Candles were lit. Ruby withdrew briefly, bounced back in her bikini. A powerful presence. I felt depressed and anxious, Harriet seemed nervous, hugged herself forlornly.

The wailing girl said, 'Oh Jesus.' The dustbin chap went red in the face. Several of the thinner people got up and left.

'What's the lady going to do?' a little girl asked her mother.

'Therapy,' said her mother.

'Like Daddy?' said the little girl.

'A different kind,' said her mother. 'Watch.'

Ruby put on a record. For atmosphere, she said. 'There was this wonderful Disney film, *Fantasia*, years ago,' she said. 'There was a part with the beginning of the world, the red sky and the steaming oceans, and then later came the dinosaurs and all. I've always loved the music.'

It was Stravinsky's *Le Sacre du Printemps*. In all the photographs I've seen of him Stravinsky looks to me like a man who was potty-trained too early and that music proves it as far as I'm concerned.

A mat was brought in and one of the bearded fellows took his shirt off and lay down on it. Ruby lay down at right angles to him and wrapped her legs round his waist. 'Let your mind go completely blank if you can,' she said. 'Breathe out when I squeeze, breathe in when I ease up. Keep looking at me.'

The muscles leaped up in Ruby's thighs, the bearded fellow gasped as the air went out of him and they were away. In about five minutes he reached YES, burst free, was happy like the people in the slides and Ruby went on to the next applicant. Nobody'd been told to bring a swimsuit, most of the men took their shirts off, some of the girls had a go in bras and knickers, others kept everything on. Ruby made a real effort with everyone, squeezing hard until they reached YES or said they had. One chap cried 'Pax!' but he was the only one. After a time I stopped paying close attention. We were all crowded round very close, Harriet's bottom was partly resting on my right hand and a bare foot belonging to one of the better-looking girls was touching my left. I felt cosy and relaxed with the candlelight, the smell of hash and sweat, the breathing and the grunting as one person after another returned to the origins of life between Ruby's muscular thighs. Even the Stravinsky became soothing with repetition.

It went on and on. I must say I rather fancied being squeezed by Ruby but I wasn't sure I felt like doing it in front of everybody. Harriet was not tempted but we were both beginning to enjoy the evening in a quiet way.

Ruby was scissors-gripping a very good-looking young man named David when he began to groan but not in the ordinary way. His eyes were closed and he seemed to be in a sort of trance. He braced his hands on Ruby's thighs and pushed as if trying to squeeze out from between her legs, worked a few inches of himself out of her grip. 'Can't breathe,' he murmured as if talking in his sleep. 'Round my neck, strangling me.'

'It's the cord,' said a blonde woman with frizzy hair and a wrinkled face. She was American too.

'What cord?' said Ruby.

'The umbilical cord,' said the blonde woman. 'I'm a therapist too. He's doing a natal, he's re-experiencing his birth. Quick, turn him, get him untangled. Loosen your grip so I can turn him.'

Ruby loosened her grip, the blonde woman rolled David round between Ruby's legs. 'There,' she said. 'That's all right now. Let him squeeze himself out the way he was doing.'

'I don't know,' said Ruby. 'This never happens back in Los Angeles. They just go back to that big YES and Zonk! They're out again.'

Murmurs and crowd noises. This wasn't Los Angeles, said several other Americans. Small stirrings of solidarity between the expatriates and those of us who were English, feelings of pride that things in London might perhaps be not quite so simple as in Los Angeles. There was renewed interest all round. David was wiggling and shimmying, parting Ruby's legs with his hands and uttering rending groans.

'Whatever it is it feels good,' said Ruby. 'It feels like something big happening. You have to stay open to whatever comes up in this kind of work.'

'He needs help,' said the blonde woman. 'I'll push from behind. Somebody else take his head and shoulders and ease him along when he tries to get himself out.'

'What are they doing now?' said the little girl to her mother.

'David's being born,' said her mother.

Willing hands were laid on at both ends of David, Ruby, and the blonde lady. More and more people joined in the delivery. By this time David, still with his eyes closed, was half way out of his trousers with all the wiggling. He was wearing black knickers. There was more pushing and pulling, much encouragement and advice, and finally with one big hoarse cry David was all the way out. Of Ruby's legs and his trousers both.

There was a general happy clamour and some of the girls had tears in their eyes. I looked at Harriet and saw that she did too. I squeezed her hand and she squeezed back. Ruby hugged David. 'Give Mommy a big kiss,' she said.

David still had his eyes closed, and as he moved into Ruby's embrace he fumbled one big bouncy breast out of her bikini top and applied himself to it like a veteran infant.

'Jesus!' said Ruby and pressed his head to her bosom. There was a spontaneous ovation from every-body except Ruby's boyfriend, who said something violent in Italian, rolled his eyes up and made a gesture. David opened his eyes and smiled a happy smile, Ruby put her breast back, somebody brought her a cup of tea. People lit cigarettes and joints, settled back cosily.

There were many earnest questions put to David by girls with glistening eyes and men in whose faces there now shone an awful lust for infancy. How had it felt, where had he been, how did he feel now? David said it had been a deep experience, it had taken him back to the darkness of the womb, his pre-natal anxie-ties, his ambivalence about his mother, his resentment of his father, his fears about coming out into the world. He told of his joy at the first light of emergence and Ruby's boob. He felt good, renewed, serene. There was less tension in his neck. That was as much as he could say now, it was something he'd have to reflect on, it had been a very deep experience.

Now there was a rush to be next for Ruby's Original Therapy but the primordial soup wasn't in it any more, being born was what everybody wanted to have a go at. Harriet put her name down on the list, I didn't. Not my time for rebirth just yet. Ruby promised to take on all comers, to go right through the night if necessary, and after a short break the therapy resumed.

Some wept as they were reborn, others raged. Some both raged and wept. The wailing girl went dead silent when she did it, the one who'd muttered to herself shouted the whole time. Stravinsky was abandoned, no one needed music any more. Additional mats were brought in to afford as it were a longer birth canal. Some thrashed about in Ruby's grip while being pulled and pushed the length of the room and others shimmied smoothly through her legs like fish. Ruby was red and blotched and chafed all over from being scraped along and struggled with up and down the room but she said that she was so energized by the atmosphere that she wasn't tired at all.

Even though many of the girls did their writhing in bras and knickers the whole thing was not sexually stimulating, everyone was in such terrible need of something harder to find than sex. I particularly noticed one impressively handsome bearded young man who had sat in a lotus position with a very straight back and a very aloof face earlier in the evening. Now he actually grovelled and whimpered waiting for his turn.

I could never have imagined Harriet squirming on a mat in the grip of a lady wrestler's legs but when her turn came there she was. She was fully clothed of course but her face was naked and I'd never seen her look like that before. I thought of films in which strange harsh voices spoke through women who were mediums. Harriet groaned and sobbed in her own voice but her body arched and twisted as if some terrible thing in her wanted to shed her like an old skin and get out. I couldn't help noticing, what with the disarray of her clothing and her skirt sliding up, that she had much more of a figure than I'd given her credit for.

By then I wasn't feeling cosy any more. One moment I was safe and a little detached and the next I looked at the candle flames and moving shadows and was sick with terror. It was as if the evening had reversed a giant devil-mirror with its picture of a world and I was silvered at the back of things, lost atoms speeding to infinity. Terror was all there was, nothing else. It might reflect the images of aeroplanes or cathedrals or Ruby in a bikini and the faces in the room but there was no reality but the terror, all that it reflected was illusion.

When Harriet had finished we left. The night outside was quiet and peaceful but the silver terror was all about us. We got a taxi and Harriet cuddled tiredly against me. Well, I thought, here we are, and took her in my arms and kissed her. When we got to her place I paid the driver, she opened the front door and we went up to her room without a word.

We took our clothes off with the terror in the room. The terror was the energy that moved us, our naked bodies moved together like the sound waves of a scream. Most animals don't make love face to face, I thought as I fell asleep. Male and female face the same way, seeing what's about them. Whales and humans show two backs to it.

26

Neaera H.

'Death of the oyster-catchers' was the heading of an article in the *Observer*:

A programme to kill 11,000 sea birds has been under way for the past month on the sands of the Burry estuary on the Gower peninsula in South Wales.

Men with shotguns have been shooting oyster-catchers on the morning and afternoon tides and, so far, several hundred have been killed. The marksmen are being paid a bounty of 25p a bird.

The South Wales Sea Fisheries Committee, which is running the culling programme, believes it is necessary to kill the birds in order to save the world-famous cockle beds of Penclawdd. The birds, they say, are eating five to six million baby cockles each winter and they can eat more in a month than the cocklers can gather in a year.

Cockling in Penclawdd, the article went on to say, was one of Britain's first forms of social security in that it offered a livelihood to women who had lost their men in mining accidents. The article ended with the words of a cockler from Crofty. 'We're having a struggle to even reach our daily quota of cockles nowadays,' he said. 'Quite simply, it is either us or the birds.'

Uncanny, I thought. Is there something keeping its eye on my mind, waiting to strike down whatever I think about? I'd never in my life seen a word about oyster-catchers in the news before. Now they're killing them. 'Us or the birds,' said the cockler.

Harry Rush's letter still lay on my desk unanswered, heavy with the burden that would be on me if I accepted. Of course I needed the £1,000, when would there ever be a time when I shouldn't? The letter nagged at me like a paper devil, I knew I'd never finish such a book if I were fool enough to start it, I'd sicken at the very first page. I had feelings of doom and damnation, utter lostness, and now the dead and dying oyster-catchers seemed to put the seal on it. Everything seemed too much for me, I was overwhelmed.

I was getting hot flashes of desperation and running about the flat picking things up and putting them down aimlessly. I wanted a rest, wanted peace, wanted the world to let me alone for a bit. *King Kong* was playing at the Chelsea Odeon, so I went.

Wonderful inside the Odeon, cool and quiet and sheltered from the world. The place had been redone, the seating was spacious and comfortable. The lights had not yet dimmed, the screen was still playing music to itself the way they always do before a film starts. I like that music whatever it is, it sounds the same in all cinemas, light and gay and full of safe expectation.

The film was first released in the United States in 1933 during the Great Depression. That sounds strange: the Great Depression. One thinks of millions of people sitting with their heads in their hands and groaning all at the same time. Many did of course but there was no atom bomb then, the world was still like a child too little to know about death. Whatever was happening beyond the camera's field of vision, innocence was still possible and one felt it in the opening of the picture: the dark and foggy harbour, the film entrepreneur with his ship bound for a secret destination, the beautiful hungry girl he recruits when he finds her stealing apples. He holds her at arm's length looking intently at her face, she returns the look almost fainting, full of surrender that is transcendentally sexual and innocent. She knows she is beautiful, knows that her beauty has been recognized, that good things will happen if she surrenders.

On the ship he rehearses her in front of the camera, has her look up ('Higher, higher!') and scream. He doesn't tell her what she'll be screaming at later but he knows he's going to bring her to some giant terror. It's a reversal of the *Schöne Mullerin* theme of the unattainable beauty: the voyeur, the picture-maker, must put his attainable beauty within easy reach of the colossal beast. I watched her scream at the unknown horror she was heading for. That was a good touch, it was absolutely right. She screamed with complete acceptance of her place in life.

When Skull Island appeared it was mostly a painted backdrop but that didn't matter; even if the studios and camera crew and all the behind-the-scenes equipment had been visible in the film it wouldn't have mattered. Even showing the animator moving his little articulated models and photographing them frame by frame wouldn't have made any difference in the effect: Kong with his teddy-bear fur is a fifty-foot tall idea even if the reality was only eighteen inches high. Kong lives. There *was* a giant arm for close-ups of Fay Wray screaming in Kong's grasp and that seems right too. Possibly somewhere in Hollywood that giant arm lies in a warehouse, empty-handed now. Kong had no visible male member even when presumably excited but then he was *all* male member in a manner of speaking so that doesn't matter either. On the other hand maybe that's why he only wanted tiny women to play with instead of looking for a fifty-foot tall she-ape with whom to have sexual kongress. The psychological ripples are ever-widening. Now that I think of it why *weren't* there any other fifty-foot high gorillas about? What had happened to Kong's mother and father? That too must be part of the pathos of the thing: Kong is an orphan and alone of his kind. Not just an orphan but a giant orphan, a monstrous Tom o'Bedlam.

Carl Denham, the film man, comes ashore with Anne Darrow (Fay Wray) and his crew to look for the legendary beast-god of Skull Island. They see the natives making ready to offer a bride to Kong. The massive wooden gates at the edge of the village suggested the size of the beast they were meant to keep out, his colossalness preceded him. There were the black men dancing in gorilla skins and chanting for Kong to come and claim his bride: 'Something something KONG! KONG! Something something KONG! KONG!' flinging up their furry arms at each KONG. The music by Max Steiner was just right. Then they saw Fay Wray and that night they went out to the ship in their boats and captured her and offered her instead of the local girl.

There she was in the light of the torches, wearing a white silk frock I think, all blonde and helpless with her head drooping and her arms outstretched, hands tied to two posts. Then she looked up, higher, higher, and screamed and screamed when Kong's luminous face rose above the trees like a giant ape-moon. It was at the same time laughable and ineffably real. Yes that's a big fake ape, ha ha. But the fake ape is only the cipher for the real thing before which we stand with outstretched arms, hands tied, head drooping, and we scream or are silent.

By the end of the film Kong too is a victim, tragic in his greatness and the height (the Empire State Building) from which he falls. When he's brought a captive to New York to be exhibited on the stage it is he who stands with arms outstretched, crucified by midgets and manacled with great thick chains.

'He was a king and a god in the world he knew,' says Denham, 'but now he comes to civilization merely a captive, a show to gratify your curiosity. Ladies and gentlemen, Kong, the Eighth Wonder of the World!'

Fay Wray is on the stage as well. When the photographers' flashbulbs go off near her Kong thinks she's in danger, he growls and strains at his chains. Then comes one of the very best lines in the film or indeed anywhere: 'Don't be alarmed, ladies and gentlemen, those chains are made of chrome steel,' says Denham. Then of course Kong breaks loose, kills some people, derails and smashes an overhead train and climbs up the Empire State Building with Fay Wray, there to be shot down by aeroplanes.

'Don't be alarmed, ladies and gentlemen, those chains are made of chrome steel.' Wonderful line. Marvellous how one's afraid of the thing that's going to break its chains and then so quickly one *is* the thing that's broken its chains and climbed the heavenward spire to be shot down.

'Oh no, it wasn't the aeroplanes,' says Denham standing by the fallen Kong (there must be a giant head in the warehouse too), 'it was Beauty killed the Beast.'

What a sad life. On his island Kong had plenty of other monsters to fight with, he was very good against the tyrannosaurus I thought. But he had no one to be friends with. Poor thing. At the end when he's dying from the aeroplanes' machine-gun bullets he reaches towards Fay Wray who's lying on a ledge where he'd put her. Weak and swaying, his grip on the spire loosening, he touches her gently, then lets go and falls. The year 1933 was full of many things. Showing with *King Kong* was a documentary film on Hitler's rise to power. In 1933 there was Goebbels officiating at a book burning. 'You do well at this midnight hour,' he said, 'to exorcise the past in these flames.' Exorcise the past. Surely that thought alone was sufficient evidence of madness. But more and more I think that madness is the world's natural condition and to expect anything else is madness compounded. In the train derailment scene in *King Kong* the engine-driver could not believe his eyes when he saw Kong's face rising through the gap where he'd torn away the tracks but that was just another day in 1933. That trains mostly stay on rails, that the streets are mostly peaceful, that the square continues green and quiet below my window is more than I have any right to expect, and it happens every day.

Madame Beetle swims in her green world expecting neither continuation nor sanity, I don't think expectation is a part of her. While there is water she will swim. Arabella spins her weightless web on *Skylab-2* and the white shark goes its way without rest. There is no buoyancy in sharks, they cannot rest, they must keep swimming till they die.

27

William G.

Sermons in stones. The other day coming home from work I noticed for the first time a manhole cover near my corner. Square plate in the pavement, K257 on it. All right, I thought as I stepped on it, go ahead, play Mozart. It didn't. When I got home I looked up K257 in the Köchel listing in my *Mozart Companion*. It was the Credo Mass in C. *Credo*. I believe. What does the manhole cover believe, or what's being believed down in the hole? I don't like getting too many messages from the things around me, it confuses me. Now whenever I walk on that manhole cover it'll say 'I believe'. When Mozart was my age he'd already been dead for eight years. I don't think I've ever heard the music.

Having slept together Harriet and I woke up together. I woke up first actually. Dora had always looked angry in her sleep. Harriet was calm and beautiful, better-looking than when awake. Lineaments of satisfied desire. I was impressed, pleased with myself as well. Maybe not a bad chap after all. Harriet kept looking beautiful when she woke up. She has quite an elegant figure too, long and graceful. Breakfast was cosy, we didn't talk much, mostly looked at each other.

That evening we had dinner together, went to my place and Harriet spent the night there. Sandor stuck his head out of his door and opened his eyes wide as she passed on her way to the bathroom. 'I believe,' said K257 as we walked over it together the next morning.

All right, I thought, I'll get through this turtle business and that'll be out of the way. I'd been giving some thought to turtle-shifting and I'd decided they could best be handled in crates. I rang up George Fairbairn and he gave me the measurements I needed. The big day would probably be in a fortnight or so, he thought. A fortnight. Right. If I'd drop off the crates first he'd have the turtles boxed and ready for pick-up. Wonderful.

Harriet was emanating weekend availability and I was more than willing but I wanted to make the turtle crates on Saturday and I wanted to keep her and the turtles separate. I told her I had things to do at home all day and evening and couldn't get over to her place until late Saturday night.

On Saturday afternoon when I finished at the shop I bought the wood for the three crates and I bought six ringbolts and a hundred feet of half-inch rope. The ringbolts and the rope are for lowering the crates or dragging them up steps or whatever. Should I have got one-inch rope I wondered. I also bought a five-gallon container for extra petrol.

Mrs Inchcliff was very pleased to see me active in the lumber-room. As soon as she heard me sawing she brought me a cup of tea. 'What're you making?' she said.

'Turtle crates,' I said. 'I'm going to steal three sea turtles from the London Zoo and put them into the sea.'

'Good,' she said. 'That's a good thing to do.'

I'd started with a hand-saw but she went to the cupboard and got out Charlie's Black & Decker power drill with a circular-saw attachment. Marvellous, the things men leave behind. Of course she'd paid for it.

'I don't know why he didn't take it with him,' she said.

'Yes you do,' I said.

'I expect I do at that,' she said. 'But he'd have been welcome to it.'

I've always been afraid of power tools. Castration complex. Castration complexes are reasonable though. More and more chances these days to have one's members lopped off by labour-saving devices as civilization progresses. All right, I thought, be a man, be powerful with a saw. So I used Charlie's Black & Decker and I didn't cut anything off after all. I was quite proud of myself. An afternoon and evening's work and there they were, three turtle crates with two ringbolts each. They were just plain open boxes, no lids, four feet long, twenty-eight inches wide, one foot deep. The turtles would lie on their backs with their flippers pressed to their sides.

'Tools,' I said. 'With tools you can do anything.'

'With tools and a man,' said Mrs Inchcliff. 'It takes both.' She'd kept me company the whole time I was working, couldn't stay away. Gave me supper too. Odd how young she looks. As far as I know she's never done anything special to keep herself young except not smoke. Maybe it's because she's never been able to get through all the stages of her life. Her youth is still in her, not lived out.

Miss Neap, back from an evening out, came down to look in on us. 'What goes in those?' she said when she saw the crates.

'Turtles,' I said. 'I'm going to put some sea turtles into the sea.'

She was standing outside the circle of the green-shaded light, her pince-nez glittered in the shadows. She had a theatre programme in her hand, fresh air and perfume had come in with her. Her blonde hair and leopardskin coat looked as if they'd go out even if she stayed at home. 'The sea,' she said. 'It always seems so far away even though the Thames goes to it.' She smiled and went upstairs.

I hadn't expected to create a sensation but I was a little surprised that Mrs Inchcliff and Miss Neap were so incurious about the turtle project. Speaking of turtles and the sea seemed to make their thoughts turn inwards.

Mr Sandor came home while Mrs Inchcliff and I were still sitting in the lumber-room admiring the crates and drinking tea. He had several foreign news-papers under his arm, was carrying his briefcase as always and smelt of his regular restaurant. 'Not strong joints,' he said looking at the corners of the crates. 'Dovetail joints better.'

'They're as strong as they need to be,' I said. I didn't say anything about turtles.

I must try to remember my first impression of Harriet, how she looked to me when I first started at the shop. Reproachful, that's what I thought. I'd said to myself quite recently that her face was a constant reproach. I mustn't forget that, however cuddly she seems now. The reproach is waiting to appear again I'm sure. I think it's always like that. Dora looked angry when I first met her and the angry look was what her face came back to in the end. And I'm sure whatever look gave Harriet her first impression of me is waiting to return to my face.

I ought to give some thought to what I'm getting

into. Casual affairs with people one works with are probably best avoided. And if this isn't a casual affair what is it? I'm not in love with Harriet. I feel good being with her, like sleeping with her, don't want to think beyond that.

It was cosy going to her place on Saturday night, walking under the street lamps looking up at lighted windows and knowing that I too had a lighted window waiting where I shouldn't be alone.

In bed we lay looking up at the patterns of light, the shapes of the windows thrown on the ceiling by the street lamps.

'What were you so busy with all afternoon and evening?' Harriet said.

'Odd jobs I'd been putting off,' I said. I thought of the first time we'd made love in this room with the terror in it, wondered if the room would slide away, the light patterns on the ceiling and the clothes on the chair, and leave only the terror. It didn't. The room stayed. Harriet was there, warm and smooth along the whole length of me. Tomorrow we'd wake up together but I couldn't tell her about the turtles.

'A penny for your thoughts,' said Harriet.

I hate it when people ask me what I'm thinking.

28

Neaera H.

I was reading about colliery horses in this morning's paper. Pit ponies, they're called. They live underground and work with the miners. They've saved lives, the article said, by stopping in their tracks and refusing to go ahead seconds before a roof-fall. They've led miners with broken lamps through black tunnels to safety, and it was said that a horse once pressed its body against a collapsing wall to give the men time to escape.

I like thinking about the horses and the men working together underground. A large strong animal and a man together add up to more than a man and an animal. They aren't afraid of the same things, and where the senses of one leave off, those of the other go on. I wish I had a horse to work with. Either I think the roof's going to fall in all the time or I think it'll never fall. I'm sure a horse would give it no thought at all except when the actuality impended. One can't have a horse to help with writing or drawing. Mice perhaps. Madame Beetle is not a help in any practical way but I feel that her attitude is exemplary. Swimming, diving, coming to the surface for air or sitting quietly in her shipwreck she is in harmony with her small world, has a good style.

How very patronizing of me, now that I consider it, to think that of Madame Beetle. If she's in harmony with her 'small world' then she's in harmony with as much of the world as she has contact with. If I enjoyed comparable harmony I'd speak of it as being with *the* world, not my 'small world'. And if I find her exemplary how can I say she's of no practical value? If I were paying a Zen master for instruction I'd consider him an exemplar whose example had practical value. Madame Beetle cost only 31p and her tiny daily fee is not even paid in money so I discount her value.

I wrote a letter to Harry Rush thanking him for his offer but saying that I simply did not have a book on The Tragic Heritage in Children's Literature in me. I wasn't sure I'd post the letter but I took it with me when I went out. I didn't feel like cooking or eating in the flat. I took Tolstoy's *The Cossacks* with me and went to an Italian restaurant in Knightsbridge near William G.'s bookshop.

It was early and the place was almost empty. I settled into a booth, ordered *escalope milanese* and a half-carafe of red and began *The Cossacks*, which I'd last read twenty-five years ago. At the end of the first short chapter I came to:

> ... the three shaggy post-horses dragged themselves out of one dark street into another, past houses he had never seen before. It seemed to Olenin that only travellers bound on a long journey ever went through such streets as these.

Perfectly true, I thought as I drank my wine. The same streets do not exist for everybody. Only travellers bound on a long journey go through such streets as those. Only solitary sojourners go through other streets, sit at tables such as this.

My seat shook a little as someone sat down in the booth behind me. I was facing away from the door and hadn't seen them come in. I went on with my Tolstoy until I heard William G.'s voice say, 'I'm having *escalope milanese.*'

'Where's that on the menu?' said a female voice, one I'd heard before. The girl at the bookshop who'd given me his address and telephone number. Her voice came from beside him rather than opposite.

'Here,' said William. Odd how people do that with menus. One person reads aloud the name of a dish and the other person requires to see it in print as if the word were a picture.

'I'll have the scampi,' she said. I didn't want to over-hear their conversation but my *escalope* hadn't come yet.

'Jannequin, Costely, Passereau, Bouzignac,' said William. 'Renaissance madrigals with soprano solo.'

'Couperin, Lully, Rameau, Baroque songs for soprano,' she said. 'I know those three but I've never heard of the others.' Probably they were on their way to the South Bank and looking at the programme.

The booth creaked as the voices became murmurous, there were silences. I concentrated on Tolstoy until my *escalope* arrived, ate as quickly as possible, finished my wine, didn't bother with a sweet or coffee. I had to pass their booth to get to the door. If they noticed me I'd say hello, if not I'd just not see them.

I passed the booth, they both looked up at me. It wasn't William G. and the girl from the bookshop. It was two people I'd never seen before.

29

William G.

I rang up a van-hire place. £2.75 per day, 2½p per mile, £10 deposit. God, how I hate the thought of driving the thing. In films people like Paul Newman and Burt Lancaster leap into vehicles they've never seen before, cars, lorries, buses, locomotives, anything at all, and away they go at speed. Sometimes they have to fight with someone first, knock him out before they can drive away. Well of course that's how it is in films. How can reality be so different?

I still haven't said anything about the turtles to Harriet and I still don't want to. She's begun saying 'We'. So-and-so wondered if we could come to a party. There was a series of early music recitals and ought we to subscribe. We went to the party, we sub-scribed to the series.

I keep waiting for the phone to ring from that other world where the turtles are. It's not another world really, it's this one. Everything happens in the same world, that's why life is so difficult. I'll pick up the van right after work, deliver the crates, come back later, meet Neaera at the Zoo and drive to Polperro. Maybe I ought to pick her up earlier, maybe we ought to have dinner first.

Yesterday evening I looked out of my window and saw the greyhound lady go past alone. No husband. The Greyhound Widow, like a figure on a tarot card.

A train went past on the far side of the common. One vertical row of three lights: Tower Hill. I knew the husband was dead, it was in the way she walked with the greyhound. I asked Mrs Inchcliff about it, she knows everything that goes on in the neighbourhood. Yes, she said, the husband had died a week ago. If he'd lived two weeks longer his widow would have got two years' salary but as it was she wouldn't.

There's an owl in the Charing Cross tube station. *Bubo tubo*. Not really an owl. The sound comes from an escalator but it's as real as the owl I hear on the common and never see. There's only one world, and animal voices must cry out from machines sometimes.

There it was: the telephone call from George Fairbairn. Thursday would be the day. This was Monday. If I could drop the crates off about half past six he'd have the turtles ready for me in half an hour or so. He was talking to me in a matter-of-fact way as if I really existed and was a real grown-up person who could drive vans, be at a certain place at a certain time and do what I'd undertaken to do. Incredible. I said I mightn't be able to get there till after seven. Right, he said, he'd see me then.

Maybe there wouldn't be a van available, maybe all the arrangements would break down. I rang up the van-hire place. Yes, I could have a van on Thursday.

Maybe I'd not be able to get away from the shop. Late summer, still lots of tourists. I asked Mr Meager if I could have Friday off. Personal matter. He said yes of course.

I thought of ringing up the Zoo and warning them that a turtle snatch was planned for Thursday. I didn't do it. All right, I thought. Let it happen.

30

Neaera H.

I hadn't posted the letter to Harry Rush, it was still in my bag. I wasn't going to do the book but nothing else was happening. Madame Beetle's good for companionship and philosophy lessons but nothing in the way of commercial profit, and Gillian Vole and that lot seem to be a thing of the past. So I wasn't completely ready to let go of the £1,000. Wasn't ready to let go of the *idea* of the £1,000. I could no more write the book than swim the Channel. Actually, with training I might in time swim the Channel but no amount of training will get that book out of me.

William G. rang up. Thursday would be the day. He spoke as if it was all really real and we were real people who were simply going to go ahead and do what we'd said we'd do. Had I in fact said it? That first day at lunch I'd talked in code, talked about hauling bananas. Had I ever said *turtles*? Yes, my very first words to him in the shop before we went to lunch. And then that awful Saturday morning when I went to his flat we talked about the turtles before I left. Perhaps I could still back out of it. But there was his voice coming out of the telephone and I said yes, Thursday would be all right. He asked if he could pick me up on his way to the Zoo with the crates and we'd have dinner before setting out. I said that would be lovely, yes of course and I'd be ready at half past six.

I looked at the telephone after I'd put it down. Sly thing, getting words out of me I'd no intention of saying. This was Monday. Tuesday Wednesday Thursday. Oh God, more than two hundred miles each way. I'll pack sandwiches and a flask of coffee but how much time will eating sandwiches and drinking coffee get us through. The whole thing is quite likely to end in disaster with the van and the turtles and us overturned in a ditch somewhere in the middle of the night, all blood and splintered glass, groans and whimpers. Maybe we'll be killed outright, and all for some stupid notion long since gone out of my head. Oh shit.

Blankets. We'll want a bit of a rest before the drive back. Pillows. Surely he won't book hotel rooms, it isn't that kind of thing. No, no, just let it be done and out of the way as quickly as possible. Towel and soap, toothbrush, toothpaste. Have a wash in the public lavatory before starting back. Wear jeans and a shirt, take a cardigan. Cigarettes, mustn't run out. Has he got maps? He looks the sort to have maps, torches, compasses. He's the anxious type and I know we'll get lost.

The tide. Will it be in or out. What's the use of bothering to find out. However it is is the way it'll be. I wonder if they're still killing oyster-catchers at Penclawdd. They must be.

I asked Webster de Vere to feed Madame Beetle, left him a key and the remains of the lamb chop she's been living on for the last week. I still haven't posted the letter to Harry Rush.

And here's Thursday.

William G.

Thursday. Grey and rainy. That was a help, sunny blue-sky days always look like bad luck to me. Harriet wanted to know where I was going but all I said was that I had things to do.

'There's no need to make a mystery of it,' she said.

'And there's no need to ask me either,' I said.

'Look,' said Harriet, 'you're perfectly free to do whatever you like ...'

'Thanks very much,' I said.

'Oh, you know what I mean,' said Harriet. 'You don't have to treat me like a stranger just because you're going to be with someone else.'

'Everything isn't sex,' I said. 'There are other things that are private.' I hadn't minded telling Mrs Inchcliff and Miss Neap but I just wasn't willing for Harriet to know everything about me. She walked away looking reproachful, had very little to say to me for the rest of the day.

After work I went to pick up the van. It was a Ford Transit 90, 18 Cwt, huge, smooth, bulgy and white, not a dent or scratch on it. I couldn't believe I'd get it there and back intact. They gave it to me with no hesitation whatever. *VANS 4-U Van Hire* in big black letters on both sides.

The man at VANS 4-U said the petrol tank held thirteen gallons and the van would do from fifteen to twenty miles to the gallon. I thought fifteen more likely than twenty although the engine certainly sounded economical, I wondered if it would go up hills with two people and three turtles. I filled the tank, later I'd fill my five-gallon container as well. On the map our route looked like about two hundred and fifty miles, and at night I couldn't count on petrol stations being open. If the van did fifteen miles to the gallon that was one hundred and ninety-five miles on a full tank and seventy-five miles more on the extra five gallons in the container, so we ought to be all right even if there were no stations open.

It felt strange sitting up so high with all that van around me. The gearbox was at least an ordinary four-speed one. The width of the thing was appalling. I was behind a bus when I first pulled out into the street and I was only about six inches narrower than it. I kept going up on the kerb with my left front wheel when I thought I was a foot away from it.

The rain was still coming down gently and steadily. I drove to my place, loaded on the crates, the trolley, the petrol container, the rope, torch, map, road atlas, an eiderdown to lie down on, an old blanket to put under it, a couple of blankets to cover us. Us? I didn't think either of us had any hanky-panky in mind and we'd have our clothes on. Couple of pillows. Thermos flask, we could probably fill it and get some sandwiches at one of the services on the M4. I felt very jumpy the whole time. Cigarettes. I took four packets. I couldn't think of anything else. I went to the loo twice, got into the van and drove off, mounting the kerb from time to time when I made left turns and getting angry looks from pedestrians. I stopped to fill the petrol container, then headed for Neaera's place.

She was waiting by the front steps when I drove up. She looked doubtful. Her basic look, I realized. Dora had looked angry, Harriet reproachful, Neaera doubtful. Not that it mattered in a permanent way, there was nothing between us except the turtles and there wasn't likely to be anything. Why not? I don't know, I think we have too much in common. We're not complementary, she doesn't fill in the blanks in me nor I in her. Both afraid of the same things maybe. We don't fit together. What if we did? There's a cheap little toy one sees at various shops, a little flat wooden clown hanging from strings between two sticks. You squeeze the sticks and the clown somersaults. His body and face are in profile and he's made so economically that one cut shapes the back of him and the front of the next clown to come from the same piece of wood. There he is with the back of his head indented by a nose-and-chin-shaped space. Looking at him one wants to fit the one behind into him and him into the one ahead. And if one fitted fifty flat wooden clowns together in a line the one at each end would still be out in the cold, one with his back and the other with his front. Fitting them together in a circle solves the problem I suppose. Then they'd just keep going round in circles.

Neaera had sandwiches and a flask of coffee in a carrier bag, pillows and blankets as well. She seemed about as nervous as I was.

'I'm not used to the width of this thing,' I said. 'It would be a help if you'd tell me when we're too close to the parked cars or the kerb.' We started off for the Zoo.

'Too close,' she said about every two minutes. I nodded and swung away, trying to think of anything

I might have forgotten. There were meant to be a spare tyre, tools and a jack somewhere in the van but I hadn't thought to ask where they were. Never mind. The rain was a nice little bonus, just enough of it to make the windscreen wipers work smoothly. I liked that, it was cosy.

George Fairbairn was on the lookout for us at the works gate, we left the crates with him and drove to a kebab house on the Finchley Road. They always play Greek music there but not too loud, just a pleasant background sound that gives privacy. I hate those places where there's a shouting kind of silence in which people make display conversation for the people listening at the other tables.

It was still light outside, the rain was coming down nicely and it was shadowy enough in the restaurant for the candle at our table to have some effect. I felt all right. Atoms speeding to infinity aren't necessarily lost, are they. They're just going where they're going. There's a thing that happens in my mind, a foreshadow of a waiting thought. Sometimes I know it's a thought that'll fill me with dread and then the dread comes before the thought. Sometimes I sense round the corner an easy thought and the ease comes. What was it, I wanted to hold on to it. Going where they're going, that was it. Things and people are as they are, where they are. Dora and Ariadne and Cyndie are where they are, Neaera and I and the turtles. That's all, nothing to be afraid of. One needn't even hold on to that, no holding on. Just let go of the terror, don't hold on to the terror. Simple if only I could remember that.

'Where is it on the menu?' said Neaera, and she laughed. I'd said I was going to have the doner kebab.

'What's funny about doner kebab?' I said.

'I was laughing because I asked you where it was on the menu,' she said. 'It's one of those odd things people always do.'

I showed it to her on the menu. We ordered a carafe of red and we both had doner kebab. Did the waiter think we were married, I wondered. I was feeling all right, smoking a cigarette and craving another cigarette at the same time but holding on to nothing else. Comfortable in a way. I'll never cease to be amazed by the fact that people uncomfortable in themselves can give comfort to other people. Even I have given comfort, Ariadne and Cyndie used to feel cosy with me. Neaera was an uncomfortable person, I could feel that. But I felt comfortable with her.

'Do you know anything?' I said.

'Not a bloody thing,' she said.

'Don't know what's best for anybody?'

'Not even for myself. Especially not for myself.'

'Wonderful,' I said. I raised my glass. 'Here's to not knowing anything.'

'I'll drink to that,' she said, and raised her glass. We both laughed, it just came out.

'Except the turtles,' I said. 'We know what's best for the turtles, eh?'

'Oh shit,' she said. No laughter. 'It seemed to want to happen, didn't it.'

'Yes,' I said. 'It seemed to want to happen.' Her face was sad. I felt at home with her face. Maybe it was a beautiful face, I don't know. It looked as tired as my own, dark circles under her eyes. Very black eyebrows, no grey in her long black hair. Harriet. Well, yes. We'd subscribed to a series of recitals but that wasn't a lifetime contract. I'd never seen Neaera's flat but I could imagine books, drawing-table, typewriter.

I could imagine being there with her in the evening reading, writing maybe.

'You haven't got a cat, have you?' I said.

'No,' she said. 'Do I look as if I've got a cat?'

'No,' I said.

'I have a water-beetle,' she said.

'Why not,' I said. 'Nothing wrong with water-beetles.'

'It started as insect exploitation,' she said. 'I thought there might be a story in her.'

'Don't reproach yourself,' I said. 'If I had anything to exploit I'd exploit it. Why should insects have special privileges, they're no better than the rest of us. We can take the beetle to Polperro as well if you like.'

'No,' she said, 'she's a fresh-water beetle and she's stuck with me, we're in it together.'

'How do you know it's a she?' I said.

'Ridged wing covers instead of smooth,' she said, 'and she doesn't have the same kind of front legs as the male. No suction pads for holding on whilst mating.'

'Male turtles have an extra claw for that,' I said.

'Nature provides,' said Neaera.

It was dark and still raining when we came out of the restaurant. We got back to the Zoo a little after eight. George Fairbairn wheeled out the crated turtles on the trolley. The turtles lay on their backs with their flippers pressed against their sides, their mouths open. I could hear them sighing, they knew they had fallen among fools. They had a fresh ocean smell.

'Got the champagne?' he said.

'Champagne,' I said.

'For the launching,' he said.

'I'll get some on the way,' I said. I hadn't thought of

such a thing as gaiety and celebration in connection with the turtles. If I can possibly miss the fun in life I'll do it.

Neaera was standing behind me and she kicked me. At the same time I realized I'd said the wrong thing. I hadn't even thought of including him. What a stupid lout I am, it's marvellous.

'I took the liberty of laying on a bottle,' he said. 'Give you and the lady a little send-off. And it's not every day I send my turtles out into the world, you know. Something of an occasion.'

Why do I always end up feeling like a child. I'm the big turtle humanitarian but he thinks of people as well. We left the turtles sighing in the van and went into the Aquarium, through the green-lit hall to the STAFF ONLY room near the entrance. We sat down at the table and he brought out the champagne. Moët-Chandon it was too. He popped the cork, it hit a photo of a lady with great big boobs that was pinned up by the duty-roster. He'd brought stemmed glasses as well and as the champagne foamed into them it did feel something of an occasion.

George Fairbairn raised his glass. We stood up with him, raised ours. 'Here's to launching,' he said. 'Anything, anywhere, any time.'

And I'd scarcely given him a thought! I felt like crying. 'Here's to you,' I said. 'Here's to the man who made this launch possible.'

'Here's to the man who pays attention to what needs to have attention paid to it,' said Neaera.

There wasn't a great deal said after that, we got through the champagne quickly, shook hands all round, promised to let him know how it had gone as soon as we got back.

How does that part in *Moby Dick* go:

Ship and boat diverged; the cold, damp night breeze blew between; a screaming gull flew overhead; the two hulls wildly rolled; we gave three heavy-hearted cheers, and blindly plunged like fate into the lone Atlantic.

Blindly plunged like fate into the lone M4.

32

Neaera H.

On our way to the M4 William stopped at an off-licence and bought a bottle of champagne. 'We owe it to the turtles,' he said. Before we started off again he showed me our route on the map. 'We stay on the M4 until after Swindon,' he said, 'then we go through Chippenham, Trowbridge, Frome, Shepton Mallet, Glastonbury, Taunton, Exeter, Plymouth, cross the Tamar, go through Looe and there's Polperro.' The rain was running down the windscreen, our heads were close together as we bent over the map, the light of the torch playing on the red and blue and green roads made me feel young again, daring and illicit after bedtime. But it was difficult to make out the place names without my reading-glasses, the map was only a beautiful abstraction.

We drove off, the windscreen wipers took up their steady beat. We were still missing kerbs and cars by scant inches on my side. 'Too close,' I kept saying as I leant away from anticipated scrapes, always expecting to hear the rending of metal. William's head was held in such a way that I knew his neck would ache before he'd been driving an hour. I don't drive, couldn't relieve him, he'd have to do it all himself.

I was determined to be alert, to take in everything and not miss anything. I continued alert on the Hammersmith Fly-over and past the Chiswick Roundabout but soon it was like concerts where I vowed to listen carefully but drifted off and dozed. I didn't actually doze in the van but fell into a sort of travel trance that alternated with an intense uneasiness about the too-closeness of everything on my side. Whatever William used to drive must have been about two feet narrower than this van. If he was still sitting in a car that wasn't there any more, was he still in his mind sitting with whoever had been in it with him? There was a long stretch of yellow lights, utterly placeless. The road seemed to come from nowhere and lead to nowhere, it seemed wholly outside of time. I listened to the hum of the engine, the hiss of the tyres, the swish of the windscreen wipers. William had said that he'd worked in advertising but he hadn't told me much else about himself.

'Were you ever married?' I said.

'Yes,' he said. He opened his mouth and I thought he was going to say more but he closed it again. Then he said, 'Were you?'

'No,' I said. I too opened my mouth, closed it again.

'Turtles,' I said, and shook my head.

'Yes,' said William. 'Turtles.'

Suddenly it seemed to me quite incomprehensible that for the last fifteen years I'd been writing and illustrating Gillian Vole, Delia Swallow and that lot. Drawing birds was what got me into it. I was working at an art studio and I'd done a little advertising campaign with cartoon birds. Somebody said I ought to try children's books and I sold my first one to Bill Sharpe. *Delia Swallow's Wedding*, that was.

A little after ten o'clock we stopped somewhere near Swindon and topped up the petrol tank. We'd done about sixty-five miles, William said, and the tank took something over three gallons. That seemed to please him, getting twenty miles to the gallon. When the van was stopped and the engine switched off we could hear the turtles breathing.

When we turned off the M4 and drove through Chippenham and the other towns William was still shaving things too close on my side. I kept saying 'Too close' and being irritated at the sound of my voice and his having to be told. This *wasn't* whatever he used to drive and this wasn't the time when he used to drive it, it was here and now and us and the turtles, damn it. There was something insulting about it, like having a man continually call you by the name of the woman he used to be with.

'Here,' I said. 'Now. Tonight. This week, this month, this year. Turtles. Us. Ford Transit 90, 18 Cwt.'

'Yes,' said William. 'Yes, yes, yes.' He knew what I meant. He changed the poise of his head, brought his neck up out of his shoulders. 'It's not too bad actually, this,' he said. 'In-between is really where I feel best. Neither here nor there.'

'There isn't any in-between,' I said. 'Any place you pass through is this moment's *here*. In-between is an illusion.'

'Thanks very much,' he said. 'You've just invalidated most of my life.'

'Mine as well,' I said. There were reflecting studs in the road shaped like crabs without legs, each with two little eyes like crabs, continually advancing out of the darkness. Each one stared at me as the van swallowed it up. I stared back.

By 11.30 we'd done a little over a hundred miles and

we stopped outside of Frome for sandwiches and coffee. The turtles breathed patiently. Crated and lying on their backs as they were they couldn't even look up at the ceiling of the van. Their ocean smell seemed fainter now, mixed with the petrol fumes from the five-gallon container. The three plastrons were pale in the light of the torch, looked heraldic: three plastrons supine on a field Ford Transit. '*Navigare necesse est. Vivere non est necesse.*'

I've seen films of newly-hatched turtles racing to the sea, whole fleets of them almost flying over the sand in their rush to the water. These three lay on their backs ponderous with the finding in them, passively waiting. Looking at them I couldn't think there was any expectation in them. When they felt themselves once more in ocean they would simply do what turtles do in ocean, their readiness was whole and undiminished in them. If permitted to live they would navigate by the sun, by chemical traces in the water, by the imprint in their genes of an ancient continent now sundered. They were compacted of finding, finding was embodied in them. There were the five gallons of petrol. I thought of the turtles burning in silence.

I got out of the van. The rain had stopped. I stood by the van, leant my forehead against the cool wet metal. The crab reflectors in the road looked at me or not as cars went past or didn't. In the pocket of my mac was the Caister two-stone. It must have been there from the last time I wore the mac, I hadn't put it there today.

33

William G.

The sky was clearing, a full moon appeared in a ragged opening in the clouds. There'd be a spring tide then, would it be in or out? I felt as if I knew about tides, felt as if I remembered them.

'I've never told you that Polperro is the place where I was born,' I said to Neaera.

'Good God,' she said. 'But when you were a child surely it wasn't how it is now?'

'I don't know,' I said. 'We left when I was a year old and I've never been back since. My mother never talked about it much. Why'd you choose it?'

'It was real once but it isn't any more,' said Neaera. 'It's souvenirs and cream teas and a box with a slot for money to preserve the character of the old Cornish fishing village. The turtles may be headed for extinction but they're real, they work. When we put them in the sea they'll do real turtle work.'

'We can't magic the whole world with three turtles,' I said.

'We'd need more?' said Neaera. 'Would a dozen do it?' We both laughed.

My mother never had said much about Polperro. She had no stories of the pilchard fishery, the huers signalling from the shore to the seine boats and that sort of thing. She was born in Calstock where her father worked at an arsenic factory until he died of it. In those days the only protection they had was lint to cover the nostrils and a handkerchief over that. My mother remembered the trees all grey and blighted near the works and the way it smelled on foggy days. She was living at home and teaching in a school but when her father died she left Calstock. Her two younger brothers were working by then, her mother had died earlier. She came to Polperro because she liked the sound of the name and she wanted to be near the sea. She used to remember the jackdaws walking on the quay among the gulls and the fishermen, how they looked as if they might speak.

She became a waitress at a tea-shop. She used to say that was the year she gave up school-teaching, Methodism and arsenic all at once. She met my father soon after and in two years she was a widow living in London with a year-old son. She bought a tobacconist-newsagent business in Fulham and then she used to get books out of the library and read about Cornwall. She liked legends and folklore. I remember her telling me about the spirit of Tregeagle who howled when the hounds of the Devil were after him and was finally sent away to weave ropes of sand by the edge of the sea. I remember how she used to say that part: 'Forever weaving ropes of sand that crumbled in his hands and the wind blew them away.'

When I think of her seeing the jackdaws walking on the quay I seem to see them with her eyes and I can see the rest of the scene as well, the grey sky over the sea and the headlands, the white-and-black-and-grey gulls with yellow beaks and yellow staring eyes, the fishermen solid and heavy in the grey light with scales and barrows, the boats rocking at their moorings or standing on their legs. I never see it sunny, always grey. I've never told anyone about my mother's jack-daws. My three uncles are dead, I have cousins in Cornwall I've never looked up. The house in Fulham where we lived over the shop until my mother died was close to where I live now but it's been pulled down, there's a block of flats there now. The road where my father went over the cliff was on the other side of Polperro, we'd not be seeing it this trip.

Near Glastonbury there was a self-service petrol station open. I put a pound note into the machine and the tank took 96p worth. 4p worth of petrol left for whoever might come along next.

The van hummed along swallowing up the little crab-shaped reflectors with their little crab eyes. The moon disappeared, reappeared as broken clouds hurried past. Oh yes, I thought, feeling something good just round the corner of my mind: just be all the way in it and you're all right. Just let go of everything like a falling star. The far-away ones, when you see their light it's already happened millions of years ago. This too, my brief light, maybe it had flashed across the darkness long long ago. Not *my* light, just a light. Now I was the one to be it, to flash across the darkness with it. Somebody else's turn next. Nothing to be selfish about, be it while it's you and then let go. The van rushed ahead but I let my mind be where it was.

34

Neaera H.

At two o'clock in the morning near Exeter William topped up the tank again. I was glad there weren't more petrol stations open. He seemed to want to arrive at Polperro with a full tank, as if he had information that all the petrol stations on the road back would disappear by morning.

At a quarter to three we had more sandwiches and coffee about twenty miles from Plymouth. We'd done two hundred miles by then, only about fifty to go. I wondered if he'd stop for petrol between here and Polperro. The road was quiet, there were long intervals between cars, I listened to the turtles breathing. Ahead of us in the lay-by a big articulated lorry was resting like a tired monster. The crabs in the road marched on inscrutably towards London. What would they say when they got there?

We went on through Plymouth, wakeful through the sleeping streets. We crossed the Tamar Bridge at half past three under bluish lights that seemed quite outside of time, like the yellow ones earlier. Lear's words about the silent-roaring ocean had got into my head and I felt myself filled with silent roaring. It may in fact have been snoring although if it was, William was too tactful to say so. I dozed off and woke up as we came down the hill into Polperro. The sky had cleared completely and there was bright moonlight over everything.

BEYOND THIS POINT ONLY EXEMPTED VEHICLES PERMITTED 9 A.M.–6 P.M., said the sign. We went beyond this point down the main street, past the model village in its model sleep, past the dark and silent cream-teas and souvenirs, turned into the street that led to Jonathan Couch's house and parked on the little bridge in front of it. We could have turned into the very narrow street that went the remaining two hundred yards or so to the outer harbour but William drew the line at that, he didn't want to risk scratching the van or waking anybody up with the noise of our manœuvres. As it was we kept expecting lights to go on, windows to fly up and policemen to appear.

We'd neither of us bothered to find out about the tide in advance. Whether it was in or out we'd launch the turtles. But I think we both felt the same: if the tide was in the ocean was with us and our venture would prosper, if it was out it meant that things were no different from the way they always were, just a lot of damned bother and aggravation. Then I stopped caring about signs and omens and whether it would go well or badly. Our part in the rhythm of things was to put the turtles in the sea and however it went would be the way it went. Getting stuck in the mud or drowning or breaking a leg or being had up by the police might or might not be part of it. I stopped caring about people waking up, I felt relaxed and invulnerable.

We rounded the corner, went down the street. The boats in the inner harbour were all afloat. 'It's in,' we both said at the same time. The wind hit us in the face, we heard the crashing of the waves as we half ran round the next corner and up the incline to the outer harbour. The low-tide beach was gone, under the full moon the tide was surging wildly against the break-water, spray was flying and the sea was breaking half way up the steps. And the wind, the wind, the full-moon spring-tide turtle wind.

Back to the van we went without a word. William dragged out the first crate, tipped it on to the trolley and wheeled it away with an amount of noise that would have waked the dead. I followed with the rope. I thought it would take both of us to get the trolley up the incline but William did it by himself. At the break-water we wrestled the crate off the trolley, laid it on the steps as on a slipway and lowered it with the rope through the ringbolts. 'Don't be alarmed, ladies and gentlemen,' I said, 'those chains are made of chrome steel.' William must have seen the film, he was laughing whilst standing on the steps with the tide breaking over his feet.

I gave him slack as he up-ended the crate on the edge of a step, he tilted it forward and with a great splash the turtle hit the water and dived. We hugged and kissed each other, ran back for the next turtle, launched it, then the next. Each one dived under the wild water and was gone. It was done, it had actually happened. Three empty crates and the turtles safely off.

'The champagne!' said William. He rushed off, came back with the bottle and the two cups from the Thermos flask. He popped the cork into the wind, the champagne foamed up in the moonlight. 'Here's wishing them luck,' we said, and drank to the turtles. The waves were silver under the moon, the spray flew up from the rocks on either side of the harbour entrance, there was a beacon on the headland. The champagne tasted like clear and bubbling bright new mornings without end. We gulped it greedily and threw the empty bottle into the ocean. The ocean was rough and real, always real, only real. It wasn't Polperro's fault that the place had to go begging with souvenirs and money-boxes and a model village. I forgave Polperro, loved it for what it had been and what it now was, for its happiness and sorrow by the sea. I forgave myself for not loving it before, loved myself for loving it now. I forgave everybody everything, felt the Caister two-stone in the pocket of my mac, flung it out into the moonlit ocean.

35

William G.

When I felt the wind on my face and saw that the tide
was in it seemed all at once that I didn't need any
answers to anything. The tide and the moon, the
beacon on the headland and the wind were so *here*, so
this, so *now* that nothing else was required. I felt free
of myself, unlumbered. Where the moon ended and I
began and which was which was of no consequence.
Everything was what it was and the awareness of it
was part of it.

The crates came out of the van and on to the trolley
easily, went up the incline smoothly, there was no
separation between crate and trolley and me and
motion. It happened, turtles happened into the ocean,
champagne happened in the moonlight.

On the way back to the big car-park we stopped at
the public lavatory. *Adamant*, said the urinal. There
was a device like the Order of the Garter but with a
lion on top. Something that looked like an owl's face
in the middle. Here, now. Coming out I listened to
the stream that runs through the village, heard
an owl quavering in the dark. Not adamant, nothing
adamant.

We pulled into the car-park, I switched off the
engine. We got into the back of the van with the
eiderdown and the blankets and the pillows. We lay
down with our clothes on, side by side with a little

space between us. First we lay on our backs then we rolled over on our sides. The space rolled over with us, stayed quietly between us all night, shaped of the front of me and the back of her.

36

Neaera H.

I woke up in the van. Ah yes, I thought, this is where I went to sleep. There was wood near my face smelling salty, oceany. Empty turtle crate. I put my ear to it, listened: silent-roaring ocean. There was rope, I touched it, licked my fingers: salt. I touched the trolley, salty as well. I rolled over, there was William still asleep. It seemed like spying to look at his sleeping face so I got out of the van.

It was afternoon. Vans with curtains in the windows were parked on either side of us and people inside them were being domestic. Refreshment and souvenir stands were open at the car-park entrance. A man with a horse and a bedizened yellow wagon half full of passengers beckoned to me like the coachman who took Pinocchio to the Land of Boobies.

Stupid really, to feel as I did just then: low-spirited and dissatisfied. There was no reason for it. We had come to Polperro to put turtles into the sea and we'd done it.

The sunlight was hot, the sky was blue. I felt all astray. At home the day and I always approached each other by slow degrees: brushing my teeth, washing my face, the first cup of coffee, the first cigarette, opening the post. Here I had nothing, just suddenly some rough beast of a day with vans and curtains and people feeding children.

Scale is a funny thing. Sometimes on hot days every-thing seems too big and spread out. Not to be grasped by the mind, not to be held in the eye. I thought of winter. Winter grey skies, winter early evenings make London small like a model town. Lighted windows in shops are like model shop windows, tobacconist, launderette, bakery. I saw the little model streets in my mind, the shops. In the model bakery a three-tiered wedding-cake, great in its tinyness. Pictures of other wedding-cakes: the '*Windsor*', the '*Paradise*', the '*Wedgwood*'. Small, small, astonishing detail in the model memory, all there to be found. The model Polperro here at Polperro was still in my mind, I com-pared it to the model London. The Polperro one was much bigger, huge and thick, not to be held in the mind or in the eye.

37

William G.

When I woke up and saw the bright sunlight the night before seemed far away and small. I was stiff and sore all over. Neaera wasn't there. I opened the doors and saw her leaning against the concrete wall of the car-park. I thought about the turtles and I couldn't believe they'd got out to sea against that heavy tide. Surely they'd been beaten back against the break-water or swept into the harbour through the gap where the boats go in and out. They were probably in the harbour now, they'd probably been picked up by fishermen.

We slowly made our way through tourists and their children to the public lavatory. I hadn't brought a toothbrush or shaving things or anything. I brushed my teeth with my finger, washed and let it go at that. Slowly and blinking in the sunlight we went to a tea-shop where we had sausages and eggs. It was while we were eating that I most felt the awkwardness of this morning after. Afternoon actually, worse than a morning. Sometimes I've felt that way after sleeping with the wrong person, and the intimacy of sex is nothing compared to the intimacy of driving two hundred and fifty miles at night and putting turtles into the sea. But it wasn't that, it wasn't that she was the wrong person for the turtles. I didn't know what it was. There seemed to be little for us to say to each other. Nothing in fact.

We walked to the harbour. The tide was out when we got there, the boats were standing on their legs or sitting on the mud. The little beach beyond the break-water displayed broken glass and contraceptives. There were some fishermen sitting on the quay and I asked them when high water had been. Seven in the morning, they said. No one said anything about turtles and there were none in sight. They must have got out to sea all right. We walked back to the car-park, got into the van and drove back to London.

38

Neaera H.

Well, then. This was the back of the turtle thing. Not quite despair as I had thought before. Just a kind of blankness, as blank and foolish as a pelmet lying face-down on the floor with all the staples showing. That's all right, a pelmet can have a front and a back, it's only a thing. A dress can have an inside and an outside. A drawing is only on one side of the paper, even a drawing by Rembrandt.

But an action, no. An action with a front and back is no good.

We drove back to London. We scarcely spoke a word. We had lunch and supper at road-side places full of motion and absence where there was ketchup in red tomato-shaped plastic bottles. The people who sat in the booths seemed to be played on a tape that erased itself. Only the motion remained, the absence. Outside on the road, inside with the ketchup. Red, heavy.

Night came but there was no rain. William only stopped for petrol once. I'd forgotten to look at the mill wheel on the inn near the car-park in Polperro. I still don't know whether or not it was turned by water that came out of a pipe.

39

William G.

Sometimes I can't believe that some mechanical happenings are only chance and nothing more. K257 in the pavement, the escalator owl at Charing Cross. At the place where we had supper on the way home I went to the lavatory. No sooner had I opened the door than there was a metallic belch and three 10p pieces leapt out of the contraceptive machine and clanged on the floor. Why, for God's sake? Why did it do it when *I* walked in? I was fully ten feet away when it happened. There was something insulting about it, contemptuous. Here, it seemed to be saying, here's a refund. Bloody cheek.

The miles rushed towards us, shot under the van. I felt absurd, couldn't find a place to put myself in relation to the three turtles now in the sea. What in the world did it all mean? Why was I in this van with this woman? Would it keep on for ever, going round and round like chewing gum on a tyre? Could it be made to stop and if it were stopped would there be anything else to do?

I had a lot of trouble with my eyes after it got dark. The road kept going abstract. Confusion, fixed and flashing. Flat shadows assumed bulk, distances lost depth, the red tail-lights of cars half a mile ahead appeared to be up in the air.

In time the Chiswick Roundabout appeared, the

Hammersmith Fly-over. It was after eleven when we got to Neaera's place. I switched off the engine and we sat there ticking over in silence for a few moments.

'Have you kept track of the expenses?' she said.

'I haven't got all the figures yet,' I said. 'I'll add it up after I take back the van tomorrow.'

'I'll ring you up,' she said, and sat there, not quite knowing how to leave. I knew she didn't want to ask me up to her flat for coffee or anything.

'There isn't any exit line for this sort of thing,' I said. 'About all you can do is shake your head and walk away kicking a stone if you have a stone to kick.'

'I've thrown my stone away,' she said. She gathered up her blankets and pillows and got out of the van. She looked in through the window. 'I shan't say anything now,' she said. She walked away without shaking her head.

I drove home, parked the van, unloaded it. Not a dent or a scratch on the great bulgy thing, I couldn't believe it. It took me a long time to get to sleep that night. I lay in bed listening to cars going down our street. I don't know why they have to go so fast, the sound of those roaring engines always fills me with rage. I kept expecting to hear one of them scrape the van. It's quite a narrow street.

40

Neaera H.

When I opened the door to my flat it was like opening a box of stale time. Old time, dead time. The windows were all closed, the place was quite airless. I opened the windows, looked out over the square. I think I've read that grains of wheat taken from Egyptian tombs have grown when planted. Wheat yes, time no. There's a mummy at the British Museum, a woman if I remember rightly, I haven't been to the Egyptian Antiquities collection for a long time. Strange, to be dead and collected. She's lying on her side in a sleeping position and as I see her in my mind she looks more alone than if she were lying formally on her back with folded hands. Her skin is old parchment, there's nothing personal about it, her bones are just bones. But her sleeping attitude is naked and private, the privacy of her sleep remains even though there's no longer a person inside it.

When I turned on the lights the night outside looked so black that I switched them off again. Shutting out the night makes it blacker. I remembered being a child out of doors in the dark of summer evenings, winter evenings, late dark and early. One saw perfectly well, it never seemed really dark until I came into the house. Then the night outside the windows would be very black.

I didn't know what to do really, didn't know how to pick up where I left off. There no longer seemed to be continuity in my life. The road went up to the turtle-launching and ended there at a chasm where the bridge was out.

I turned on the light in Madame Beetle's tank. There were snails in the tank, red ones, six or seven of them. They were cleaning up the algae, there were little clear meanders on the glass where they'd been working. Yesterday's and today's meat lay pale and wan on the bottom. The snails were working on that as well. Madame Beetle was in the corner of the tank under the filter sponge. There was a note under the china bathing beauty, I read it by the light of the tank:

> Took the liberty of dropping in
> a clean-up squad. Can take them
> back if you don't want them.
> > Best wishes,
> > WEBSTER DE VERE

Cheek, I thought. If I wanted to run a dirty aquarium that was my business. Come to think of it Madame Beetle was a predator, why hadn't she had a go at the snails? Tired maybe.

I looked in my bag for cigarettes and there was the letter to Harry Rush still unposted. I lit a cigarette, went out of the flat and down to the corner. There are two telephone kiosks and a pillar box there. The telephone kiosks aren't the same size, one of them's larger and more heavily built than the other. I always think of them as bull and cow. They stood there, red in the dark, dark in the light of the street lamp, the bull telephone and the cow telephone and the pillar box. None of them said a word as I pushed the letter through the slot and it dived into the dark. Goodbye £1,000. It was never really there.

41

William G.

I woke up. There you are, I thought: life goes on. There was an old German film I saw at the National Film Theatre, Harry Bauer was in it. Massive man, head like a bald granite statue. In the film he was in prison for a long stretch, twelve years I think. He marked off the days on the wall of his cell with a bit of charcoal. When he got to the half-way mark he threw back his head and let out a hoarse cry. I thought of trying a hoarse cry, decided not to. Anyhow I was past the half-way point.

Saturday it was. Nine o'clock. I looked out of the window. The day was grey and wet. Harriet would be on her way to the shop. My mind turned away from everything all at once. I realized at that moment that the end of all things need not be difficult. No effort of any kind, just a turning away by whatever means might come to hand.

I went to the bathroom. Sandor hadn't cleaned the bath. A ring of Sandor dirt round it, Sandor pubic hair. Rage coursed through my veins. I'd had a whole life, a house and a family! And it had come to this: Sandor's pubic hair in a rented bath.

I cleaned the bath, had a bath, shaved even though it was Saturday. Dressed, went to make my breakfast. Sandor'd left the cooker filthy and evil-smelling as usual.

I went down the hall, knocked on his door. I was shaking all over. Sandor opened the door. He was in his dressing-gown, some lurid Persian-looking thing. He was wearing red velvet slippers that made his feet look very white, the hair on his ankles very black. His feet turned out as if there were no limit to the amount of space they could take up.

'Too much!' I heard myself saying. 'Too much!' I said it again.

'What you mean?' said Sandor, filling up the doorway and growing larger. His breath smelt the same as the cooker. Squid? Kelp? Goat hair?

'Too much!' I said again like some clockwork idiot.

'What?' said Sandor with a very red face and a very black moustache. 'What the devil you mean?'

'You clean that cooker,' I said.

'What clean cooker? Who say?' said Sandor. More breath.

'*You* clean cooker, *I* say.' I poked him in the chest with my finger. Springy chest, great deal of hair.

'Mind,' he said. 'Go slow, I caution you. Piss off. All best.'

'No,' I said. 'Not all best. All bleeding worst. Clean that cooker right now.' I grabbed him by the lapels of his dressing-gown. I was quite surprised to see my hands shoot out and do it. Thin wrists.

'Aha!' said Sandor. 'You better don't make trouble, you.' *His* hands shot out. *Thick* wrists. All of a sudden I was turned round with my left arm twisted up behind my back. I flung my right arm back as hard as I could and caught him in the face, then we were both on the floor and he had me in, yes, a scissors grip. I started to laugh but lost valuable breath doing it. What a terrible pong he had. His personal smell, no amount of bathing would have helped. He tightened his legs and I felt all my ribs crack. I might have known that a man with a moustache and an accent like that would be an accomplished wrestler. I wished I'd waited till he'd got his trousers on, he was only wearing underpants and I hated having his bare legs round me.

We'd fallen out of his doorway into the hall. My face was on the musty threadbare carpet, one ear pressed to the silence of the carpet, the other listening to Sandor's heavy breathing as he squeezed harder. A train went by on the far side of the common and in my mind I saw it under the wet grey sky, under the trailing edges of grey cloud drifting, the single clatter of the train as lonely, as only as a trawler out at sea, the only diesel putter on the wide grey sea with silence all round as far as the eye could see.

In my mind I saw the wet iron rails receding Putney-wards, cold wet iron in the rain, red lights, green lights shining on the iron, shining red, shining green, fixed and flashing, no confusion. The rails led very likely to Port Liberty. That was my mistake, I'd always thought a sea approach and never thought how very iron and wet the rails were. Tower Hill, the lights would say that passed beyond the trees along the common, Upminster or Edgware. I could see in my mind the grey and rainy air over the trains, over the common, in between the branches of the trees. I stretched out my hands, thought of holding the grey air cool and wet in my hands.

I'd been wrong to feel my past no longer mine. I was joined umbilically to all pasts but why labour it. Squeezing was all very well, the question was: did one in fact want to come out. Was one willing. To be. For whom was the effort being made? Not the untold jackdaws walking on the quay, I wasn't going to believe that. I'd asked a straight question and I wanted a straight answer. Was it for her? Was it for him? I didn't think it was for me. Go ahead and squeeze, I thought. I'm not coming out just because you want me out. It bloody isn't for me.

Not for me at all. On the other hand what was. For anybody. Nothing really. Not for her when she came out and not for him. Nor would my coming-out be for anyone whatever they might think. In that case why hold on to me. A futile gesture. Life went on, one couldn't stop half way. I was getting angry. There was a redness silently exploding in my mind. Violence. Lovely. Bumpitty bump.

I was on the landing feeling quite wrenched and pulled about. Mr Sandor was one flight down, rubbing himself in various places and looking up at me with great concentration. Now he's *really* going to be angry, I thought. I didn't mind. I didn't care if we killed each other.

Mrs Inchcliff came racing up the stairs. She'd never smoked, stairs were nothing to her even at sixty. 'What's happening?' she said. 'Why is everyone lying on the floor? Are you both all right?'

'We have collision,' said Sandor. 'Down we tumble.' He was still staring at me and I saw in his face that he saw in my face that I wasn't afraid of him any more.

Later I drove the van back to VANS 4-U. Five hundred and fifteen miles without a dent or a scratch! I was tremendously impressed by that. The shape of the van was so different from the shape of me and my life, how had we managed to stick together without hitting anything for all those miles!

42

Neaera H.

Something very slowly, very dimly has been working in my mind and now is clear to me: there are no incidences, there are only coincidences. When a photograph in a newspaper is looked at closely one can see the single half-tone dots it's made of. There one sees the incidence of a single dot, there another and another. Thousands of them coinciding make the face, the house, the tree, the whole picture. Every picture is a pattern of coincidence unrecognizable in the single dot. Each incidence of anything in life is just a single dot and my face is so close to that dot that I can't see what it's part of. I shall never be able to stand back far enough to see the whole picture. I shall die in blind ignorance and rage.

The men who used to work in the hole in the street are gone, the hole is closed up. I don't know if the street is different or not. In the shop where I'd seen the oyster-catcher on TV all the screens showed two men in sombreros shooting at each other with revolvers from behind rocks.

I passed an antique shop. There was a brown and varnished sea-turtle shell in the window. A black man — was he from the Caribbean? — was looking at it. He wore a white mac, it was a wet grey day. Next door was a fruiterer, there were oranges. The rain stopped, the sun came out into a gunmetal sky. 'Well, yes,' I said aloud. 'Of course.'

The black man turned and looked at me. 'Tortuguero,' he said. He said it like a password but made no secret sign. He said it because he needed to say the name aloud just there and then to me. I nodded, felt dizzy with my face against the dot. How did he know that I knew where Tortuguero was? I shall never see the picture. I could grind my teeth and weep.

On my desk in the middle of the night does some tiny figure look at Madame Beetle and dream of setting her free? Is there any limit to smallness and largeness? Is it possible actually to hold an orange in the hand? Iron and wind are both grey. Would there be oyster-catchers in armour on the rooftops if I looked up?

The sea was wherever it was, and the turtles. It couldn't be done again. Of those who did the launching there were no survivors. I passed an empty playground. The rocking horse was rocking, all its five seats empty.

I went to the Zoo, to the Aquarium. The turtle tank was empty, still being cleaned. I opened one of the PRIVATE doors, found George Fairbairn on the duckboards behind the fish tanks. There was a clean ocean smell, the illuminated water seemed like clear green time, the wood of the duckboards was like the wood in boats.

'Well,' he said, 'they get off all right?'

'Yes,' I said, 'they must have done, unless you've heard any reports of turtles being picked up off the Cornish coast.'

'Not so far,' he said.

I had nothing to say but I felt safe on the boat-feeling wood in the green light of salt-water time.

'All right?' he said. 'You look a little peaky. Fancy a cup of tea?'

'I'd just like to stay here a while and look at the water,' I said.

'I'll bring it here,' he said.

Below me the leopard shark swam his aimless urgent round like an office boy. Twit, I thought.

George Fairbairn came back with the tea-tray, set it down on a plank. I'd never really looked at him closely, he didn't compel attention. He was a very medium-looking man, neither tall nor short, neither dark nor fair, about my age. His face was just a plain face, cheerful and undemanding.

'How do you stay cheerful?' I said.

'I don't mind being alive,' he said. He poured the tea, took a tin of tobacco out of his pocket, rolled a cigarette, lit it. 'There's nothing you can do about this, you know,' he said. 'Nothing to be done really about animals. Anything you do looks foolish. The answer isn't in us. It's almost as if we're put here on earth to show how silly they aren't. I don't mind. I just like being around them.'

I began to cry. I leant against him and sobbed.

'It's all right,' he said, stroking my hair. 'You needn't hold back, these are all salt-water tanks.'

43

William G.

There's nothing like a little physical violence to make a man feel young again. I was half crippled from it. Sandor must have trodden heavily on my left foot, the next morning it was so tender and swollen that I could hardly put my weight on it. My ribs felt as if I'd been run over by a lorry, my left arm and shoulder weren't working right, my neck was stiff and sore and the left side of my head felt soft.

The cooker was clean when I got to it to make breakfast but I was sure that was only because it was Sunday and Sandor was sleeping in. I doubted very much that I'd find it clean on Monday morning. I spent a quiet day with the newspapers, went to a Japanese film at the National Film Theatre in the evening, took a late walk. Harriet rang up while I was out but I didn't phone her when I got home. I had Monday morning, the bath and the cooker on my mind. In bed I lay awake for a long time with fantasies of beating Sandor into a state of abject obedience but the fact was that I couldn't do it. He was younger and bigger and stronger than I and he handled himself very well indeed. I thought of getting up earlier so as to be first at the bath and the cooker which would leave Miss Neap to follow him. She'd see to him. But that would be cheating.

Monday morning I woke up early. A grey and

dreary morning with no hope in it. Things would always be the way they were, it said. Why struggle. I thought of the dawn wind over the ocean. 'Out at sea the dawn wind/Wrinkles and slides,' said Eliot. I took *Four Quartets* off the shelf and looked at *East Coker*. It begins with 'In the beginning is my end.' The line I'd remembered was at the end of Part I:

Dawn points, and another day
Prepares for heat and silence. Out at sea the dawn wind
Wrinkles and slides. I am here
Or there, or elsewhere. In my beginning.

Towards the end of the poem I read:

There is only the fight to recover what has been
    lost
And found and lost again and again: and now,
    under conditions
That seem unpropitious. But perhaps neither gain
    nor loss.
For us, there is only the trying. The rest is not our
    business.

The last words were:

In my end is my beginning.

All this for Sandor's ring round the bath and his muck on the cooker. Ridiculous. But so is everything. So was Thermopylae. The things that matter don't necessarily make sense. My end seemed immanent in every breath and my beginning seemed never to have happened.

The turtles would be well on their way now, following whatever track they followed. Just doing it. Not thinking about it, just doing it.

No sound from the bathroom. Sandor didn't have a

bath every morning. I heard his door open, heard him padding to the kitchen, heard and smelled his cooking, heard him go back to his room.

I dressed, went to the kitchen. Muck all over the cooker again. I got the cloth that I always cleaned it with, held it under the cold tap, got it good and wet, knocked on Sandor's door.

'Who is it?' said his voice from inside.

'Me,' I said.

He opened the door. Persian dressing-gown, red slippers, hairy ankles.

I held up the wet cloth. 'Clean the cooker,' I said.

'I clean your cooker right enough,' he said. 'I break your bones, you don't go away.'

I shoved the cloth into his face, brought my knee up hard into his crutch. When he doubled over I got both hands on his head, forced it down as I brought my knee up again into his face. What am I doing, I thought. He'll kill me for sure this time.

He was on the floor with blood all over his face and I thought it might be wise to beat him unconscious if I could but before I could get in another blow his feet shot out and I went flying. Slammed into the wall and that was the last I knew for a while.

When I came to I was on my bed and Mrs Inchcliff was sitting by me. 'Where's Sandor?' I said.

'He's gone off to the doctor to get his nose seen to,' she said.

'How'd I get here?' I said.

'We carried you,' she said. 'Mr Sandor and I. What *is* all this between you two?'

'It's nothing,' I said. 'Thermopylae. In my end is my beginning.'

So I came limping into the shop rather late and there

were all those books and Mr Meager and Harriet selling books and customers buying books and I thought, What in the world am I doing here, what's all this nonsense with books and who are these people? As I came in through the door the books and people seemed to get farther away instead of closer, receding from me as the shore recedes from a boat that sails away.

'Got everything sorted out all right?' said Mr Meager.

'Yes,' I said, 'thank you. Sorry I'm late, it couldn't be helped.'

'Feeling all right?' he said. 'You look a bit off this morning.'

'No more than usual,' I said. 'It's just that you haven't seen me for a few days. You probably don't notice how I look ordinarily.' My mind seemed clear but my head felt a funny shape. I turned to look at him from the hard side of it. He looked back at me with his whole head nice and hard. He has very bright blue eyes like Paul Newman but nobody would ever buy a poster of Mr Meager.

Harriet brought me a mug of coffee with a manner that seemed unnecessarily domestic. She looked heavily understanding, which irritated me. I felt there wasn't anything to be understood. And my head really did hurt where I'd hit the wall with it.

'I rang you up last night,' she said, 'but you were out.' There was the reproachful look again, the same look I'd seen when I first met her.

'I got home too late to ring you back,' I said.

'How are you?' she said very seriously as if I'd just come back from hospital.

'I'm fine,' I said, and she looked hurt. You can tell

me, her eyes said. No, I couldn't tell her. What was there to tell? You can't do it with turtles, that's all. You have to fight Mr Sandor and everything else. Every day, every inch of the way.

'You can't do it with turtles,' I said.

'You can do it with me,' she said, and gave me a quick grope behind the counter. The singlemindedness of the woman!

'That's not the only it there is,' I said.

'*Sorry*,' said Harriet, and removed herself to the Occult section.

I rang up Neaera when I had a moment. She wasn't home.

At lunch-time I went to Hyde Park and ate my sandwich and apple under a tree and did not give up smoking. Soon maybe but not yet. I looked at the yellow leaves on the grass and the boats on the Serpentine and the people around me as if I'd come back from the Lakes and the Torrible Zone and the hills of the Chankly Bore. But nobody said how tall I'd grown. All the yellow leaves were too much for me, I didn't know if I could go back to the shop and last the day out.

I did last the day out. Just. In the afternoon Harriet said, 'Will you be over this evening?'

'Harriet ...' I said.

'God,' she said, 'you sound so *weary*.'

'I'm pretty thin on the ground right now,' I said. 'There's not all that much of me. I need to be by myself.'

'Well, good luck to you and all the best,' she said, and quickly sold a Knightsbridge lady *Rising Sap*, by Taura Strong.

44

Neaera H.

Things appear from unexpected quarters. The single dot before the face becomes another dot of different shape and density.

George Fairbairn had been a background person until now. Now he was the dot before my face, the face before my face. Knowing that I should never see the whole picture I didn't bother to ask myself what it was.

He had seemed so medium, so unspecially placed between the top and bottom of life that I hadn't really given him full human recognition until that evening when he brought out the champagne. I'd assumed that he was married, part of a closed circle, no lines moving on his map.

He wasn't married. He had a flat off Haverstock Hill and that's where I woke up on Tuesday, the morning after I'd gone to see him at the Aquarium. There was very little in the place, mostly it was furnished with light and quiet. It was on the top floor and looked out over rooftops. There was a Chinese teapot in the kitchen, there was a copy of Lilly's *The Mind of the Dolphin* on the table by the bed. In the sitting room were R. H. Blyth's four volumes on haiku and some natural history. 'I don't buy books much any more,' he said. There was a radio but no gramophone.

A curious man, somewhat off to one side of things. As he said, he didn't mind being alive but I don't think it meant a great deal to him. I asked him nothing about himself and he offered no information, that was how it was. He had a clean look and a clean clear feel, nothing muddy. That was enough. There was about him the smell or maybe just the idea of dry grass warm in the sun.

He made breakfast for us. Looking out of the window and across a lawn I saw other people having breakfast in their windows.

'Do you think you'll go on doing children's books?' he said.

'I don't know,' I said.

We left the flat. In the lift at the Belsize Park tube station there was a Dale Carnegie poster. MAXIMISE YOUR POTENTIAL, it said, and showed a drawing of a thick-faced man in simplified light and shade. He had a pencil poised in his hand and stood looking down at a graph on his desk. Whether you read the graph from his side of the desk or mine the line on it went down.

At Camden Town George kissed me and got out of the train. I went home to Madame Beetle and the snails.

45

William G.

Tuesday morning. I woke up and groaned. I ached all over, and when I got out of bed I could scarcely walk. If Sandor was going to fling down the gauntlet again I didn't know whether I had the strength to pick it up.

The bath was clean. The cooker was clean. What had happened to Sandor? He was as regular as clockwork, never overslept. Had I done him a serious injury? For a moment I hoped so, then I hoped not. I knocked on his door. No answer. I knocked again, looked at the threadbare musty carpet where my face had been the other day, heard a train go past beyond the common.

'Who is it?' said Sandor's voice from inside, a little more distant than last time.

'Me,' I said. 'Are you all right?'

'Come in,' he said. He was in bed wearing some sort of wild Islamic pyjamas. He had a sticking-plaster across his nose, his face was flushed, his moustache looked dismayed. There were stacks of foreign newspapers, a chessboard with the pieces standing on it in the middle of a game, flowers in an *art nouveau* vase that incorporated a naked lady. There were framed photographs of men with moustaches, sad-faced women, young Sandor in shorts and a jersey with some school team, a river with a bridge. The wallpaper was old and dark, the furniture was dark, the room had a dark and foreign smell. There was a thermometer in a glass on the bedside table.

'Are you all right?' I said. He looked as if he might be wearing a nightcap but wasn't.

'I am grotty a little,' he said. 'I have 39 degrees temperature, maybe a touch of influenza.'

'Have you had breakfast?' I said.

'I have slightly vertigo,' he said. 'I stand up, room goes round, floor is slanty. Not hungry.'

'I'll make you some tea and toast,' I said.

'Not to bother,' said Sandor. 'I get up later.'

'It's no bother,' I said.

'Very kind of you,' he said. 'You are pacific this morning. You don't make aggression.'

'I don't usually make aggression,' I said. I made the tea and toast, brought it to him.

'What do you usually have for breakfast?' I said.

'Half grapefruit,' he said. 'Seaweed, squid, coffee. Very healthy. Top protein.'

I nodded. Cookers simply have to take what comes to them, that's life.

'You don't like foreigners, yes?' he said. 'England for the English. You don't like foreign breakfast on cooker. Not nice, yes?'

'I don't dislike foreigners,' I said. 'You've got the wrong idea completely.'

'Cobblers,' said Sandor. 'You make effort, put fake smile on face, make politeness. You nod hello but you don't look at foreigner like regular human person. You look at me as if you think I carry in my briefcase nothing but sausages.'

'What *do* you carry in your briefcase?' I said.

'Sausages and newspapers,' he said. 'I read and speak Hungarian, Russian, German, French, English. How many languages do you have?'

'Only English,' I said.

'Wonderful,' said Sandor. 'Let the rest of the world learn to talk to you. You don't waste your time with such foolishness.'

'Maybe not,' I said, 'but I leave the bath and the cooker clean for the next chap, the next human person. I'd better be going now or I'll be late for work.'

Sandor lay back on his pillow, closed his eyes. 'Thank you for your visit,' he said.

46

Neaera H.

When I got back to my flat after leaving George Fairbairn the sky went hard and blue, the sun came out in real postcard style. I didn't like it. Sunny days have always been more difficult for me than grey ones.

The snails grazed slowly on the sides of Madame Beetle's tank, the little china bathing beauty turned her back on them, Madame Beetle stayed under the filter sponge. Everything seemed stupid. I walked about from room to room, took books from shelves and put them back, dug up old letters and read lines here and there.

The place seemed suddenly intolerably full of things. The cupboards were bursting with clothes and shoes I'd never wear again, the drawers were full of rubbish, the files choked with defunct correspondence.

I began to thin out my belongings, tied up clothes in bundles, stacked old newspapers, filled carrier bags with what had filled the drawers. Then I felt exhausted, had some lunch, drank coffee, smoked.

I didn't want to be in my flat for the rest of the day. I put some paper in a file envelope and went to the British Museum. I sat on a wooden bench on the porch. Pigeons and tourists were active all round, the sunlight seemed tolerable there. I held the envelope on my lap, feeling the weight and thickness of the blank paper inside. I closed my eyes, thought of all the years of

Gillian Vole, Delia Swallow and the other animals and birds I'd written about and drawn. They led such cosy cheerful lives, that lot. I'd written them but there no longer seemed a place in their world for me.

With my eyes closed I could still see the sunlight. For a moment I saw ocean, sharp and real, the heaving of the open sea, the sunlight dancing in a million dazzling points. The turtles would be swimming, swimming. It *had* been a good thing to do and not a foolish one. Thinking about the turtles I could feel the action of their swimming, the muscle contractions that drove the flippers through the green water. All they had was themselves but they would keep going until they found what was in them to find. In them was the place they were swimming to, and at the end of their swimming it would loom up out of the sea, real, solid, no illusion. They could be stopped of course, they might be killed by sharks or fishermen but they would die on the way to where they wanted to be. I'd never know if they'd got there or not, for me they would always be swimming.

I was in my ocean, this was the only ocean there was for me, the dry streets of London and my square without a fountain. No one could make me freer by putting me somewhere else. I had as much as the turtles: myself. At least I too could die on the way to where I wanted to be. Gillian Vole! Not enough, not nearly enough.

I took paper out of the envelope, took a pen out of my bag. What was there to write? Anything, everything:

Madame Water-Beetle lived in a plastic shipwreck in a tank by the window. In the same tank lived seven red snails. The snails did the snail work and she did the beetle work.

The perversity of the human mind! I folded the sheet in half, put a fresh one on top of the stack, sat there with it blank for a long time. I wished I had somewhere to go besides my flat. Somewhere bright and empty with uncluttered shadows, somewhere not crusted with years of me. Like George's place.

47

William G.

Sandor stopped in bed Tuesday, Wednesday and Thursday, and for those three days I found the bath and cooker clean every morning. If he used the cooker at odd times when I was out there was no evidence of it. Maybe Mrs Inchcliff was looking after him. And of course he wasn't buying fresh supplies of squid and seaweed while he was laid up. Maybe he was cooking things that left no trace. I wasn't quite interested enough to visit him again.

Friday he was up and about again. The bath was almost clean, only a hair or two. The cooker was just that tiny bit mucky but without the usual smell. Well, I couldn't make a career of it really. The two fights had been sufficient satisfaction, or almost. I could fight Sandor every day and maybe even win now and again by foul means if not fair but I had no way of forcing him to clean the bath and the cooker.

At the shop Harriet and I were polite to each other. It had come to that. Instead of brushing against each other and touching as often as possible we now avoided contact like thieves wary of a burglar alarm. With no prospect of getting her clothes off again I found the thought of her naked charms vivid in my mind from time to time but I didn't want to be half of the 'We' who did this and that and were invited here and there. I didn't want to be expected anywhere as a regular thing. I didn't fancy any more early music either, and there were still two recitals left in the series we'd subscribed to. I'd give her the tickets, she could find someone else to go with easily enough.

On Tuesday I'd rung Neaera up to tell her what our expenses had been. The van and the petrol had come to £26.56, which made her share £13.28. The crates and the rope were on me. 'We promised George Fairbairn a report of the expedition,' I said. 'Maybe we ought to drop in at the Aquarium one day soon.'

'I have done,' she said. 'But I'm sure he'd like a visit from you as well.'

I went to see him on Saturday. The two small remaining turtles were back in the tank now, they looked like orphans. Well, I thought, take care of yourselves and grow big and maybe one day somebody will take you to Polperro.

'Anybody say anything yet?' I asked George.

'Nobody's been,' he said, 'except the blokes who work with me. Nobody from the Society.'

'Maybe nothing'll happen at all,' I said. 'Is that possible?'

'It's what I expect,' he said.

Well, I hadn't done it to make the headlines. Still I would have thought *some* notice would be taken in this part of the world at least.

He gave me a cup of tea in STAFF ONLY. The lady with the big boobs smiled from her photo by the duty-roster. No champagne today. It occurred to me just then that I could have brought him a thank-you bottle of something but of course I hadn't. I never miss.

'How're you feeling now that you've done it?' he said.

I shrugged. 'I think the turtles are better off,' I said, 'which was after all the object of the exercise.'

'But?' he said.

'You know how it is,' I said. 'Launching the turtles didn't launch me. You can't do it with turtles.' Why was I talking to him like a son to a father. He wasn't older than I or wiser. Just calmer.

'You can't do it with turtles,' he said. 'But with people you never know straightaway what does what. Maybe launching them *did* launch you but you don't know it yet.'

'How's Neaera?' I said. 'She said she'd been to see you. I haven't seen her since we got back.'

'She's all right,' he said, and rolled a cigarette. He did it very deftly, it was a nice smooth cigarette.

'You think it's launched her?' I said.

'Hard to say,' he said.

We finished our tea and I left. There were friendly feelings on both sides but neither of us urged the other to stay in touch.

48

Neaera H.

I came home from the museum on Tuesday having written nothing but that Madame Beetle paragraph. I looked at the telephone and said, 'Ring'. It rang but it wasn't George, it was William phoning to tell me what our expenses had been. Then in a few minutes it rang again and it was George. He invited me out to dinner and I asked him to my place for drinks first.

The flat looked different with that to look forward to. Everything in it, all the clutter on the desk and the drawing-table, all the books and objects took on new character with the prospect of being seen by him.

I bought whisky and gin and flowers. I had a long bubble-bath, washed my hair, put on the Arab dress I look best in and my posh boots. Patchouli too. I'd bought it for the first time only the other day at Forbidden Fruit but it seemed as if it'd always been my scent.

There was a knock on the door about an hour before George was due.

'Good evening,' said Webster de Vere. 'I hope I'm not disturbing you. Were you in full flow at the typewriter?'

'Like a river in spate,' I said, certain for no particular reason that he'd listened at the door before knocking.

'I mustn't bother you then,' he said with a good deal

of optical activity. Such bright glances! I said nothing, stood at the door without asking him in. He *was* bothering me. 'But I thought,' he said, 'perhaps you might be persuaded to abandon your muse briefly for a sherry with me. Dreadful, really, we've been neighbours all these years and yet we scarcely know each other.'

'I don't think it's dreadful at all,' I said. 'A friendly presence scarcely known can be quite nice.' I hadn't meant that to be encouraging but it encouraged him.

'Then you'll come,' he said, his eyes absolutely darting rays of light.

'Thank you,' I said, 'but I can't. I'm expecting someone in a little while.'

'Pity,' he said, lowering his sparkle. 'Another time perhaps. How're the snails?'

'Cleaning up,' I said, moving back a little with my hand on the door.

'Actually they have tiny wireless transmitters in them,' he said with an evil smile. 'So I get to know everything that goes on in your flat.'

'I'm afraid it must be terribly dull listening for you,' I said. 'You must excuse me now.'

'Till soon,' he said as I closed the door.

I quickly took the snails out of the tank, put them in a peanut-butter jar full of water and left the jar outside his door.

What could have worked him up to that awful pitch? He'd seen me often enough without getting all excited. But until he fed Madame Beetle he hadn't seen my flat which perhaps looked as if a good deal of work was being done and a comfortable living being made. Maybe he was tired of young men and old ladies and wanted to settle down. Dreadful of me to think it but I thought it.

'There's a jar of snails outside your neighbour's door,' said George when he arrived.

'I know,' I said. 'They were in Madame Beetle's tank for a while but I didn't like the way they looked at me.'

'There'll be more,' he said, and showed me little patches of eggs on the sides of the tank.

'That's all right,' I said. 'I'll get them before they get me.'

He walked about the flat looking at things. I'd only seen him in shirtsleeves before. He was wearing an old tweed jacket with leather patches on the elbows, no tie.

'You look different tonight,' he said.

'How?' I said.

'Jolly. Full of smiles.'

'That's how I feel,' I said. We both drank gin neat, it was bright and velvety. We smiled at each other over our glasses, time seemed full and easy, available in unlimited amounts. George seemed to carry a clear space about with him that made all things plain and simple where he was. The room lost its tired complexity, became comradely and cheerful. Without going to the window I knew that the evening view of the lamplit square would be as round and juicy as a ripe plum.

We went to the Bistingo on the King's Road and had steak and drank red wine. The evening seemed very bright. We walked up the Embankment to Westminster afterwards, then over the bridge to the South Bank. We walked about on the different levels up and down the steps and by the river. The plaza by the Royal Festival Hall was like a gigantic stage-set, the night was full of quiet excitement, the river was shining, the music-boats had gemmed windows, the trains across the Hungerford Bridge were freighted with promise.

We had coffee at the National Film Theatre clubroom, then walked back to my place slowly and by devious routes. At two o'clock in the morning we came past the Albert Bridge. Five or six taxis always park there for the night by a little hut that must be a dispatcher's office. In the first taxi in the rank the driver was sitting in the back seat in the dark playing a muted trumpet. Dixieland. The music floated quietly through the open window, small and lively.

'What is it?' I said.

'*Muskrat Ramble*,' said George.

At home we lay in bed smoking, watched the shapes of light on the ceiling, pale abstractions from the street lamps.

Before I fell asleep I saw green water, the white shark-glimmer. I looked at my watch. Half past three. I hope William's all right, I thought.

49

William G.

Sundays come round so quickly, sometimes there scarcely seems a day between them let alone a week. My mother had at least had the Methodist Church to go to and to stop going to, either way it was a positive action. I had nothing except a strong feeling of dread. Perhaps my mother had had that as well. I remembered it from earliest childhood, the awful Sunday daylight through the coloured glass of the front door, the quiet outside.

Sunday is the day when there you are with the people you live with and that's it. Or there you are alone. There'd been Sundays when I'd methodically picked up girls at the Victoria & Albert or the British Museum, Sundays drove strangers into each other's arms. But I simply hadn't that much enterprise now. I thought of Port Liberty but didn't fancy the trip to Greenwich. I decided to have a lazy day, maybe Sunday would just take care of itself and not bother me.

Sandor invariably went out on Sundays looking just like the rest of the week except no tie. He even carried his briefcase and I suppose he went somewhere where everybody spoke five languages and read many newspapers and argued about politics all day.

Miss Neap either solved or compounded the weekend problem at least once a month by visiting her mother in Leeds. At other times she maintained a full

Sunday cultural schedule and working as she did at a ticket agency was never without something to do. She was an avid museum-goer in the afternoons and favoured music in the evenings, overdressing smartly and appropriately for each part of the day.

Mrs Inchcliff was out scavenging as usual. I believe Sunday was her building-site day, she tended to bring home new-looking timber and sometimes clean bricks, all to be hoarded in the lumber-room, perhaps against the advent of a new friend handy with tools.

So I had the place to myself, and from my window looked out across the common where the trains clattered by and the shining rails maintained their perspective vanishing towards Putney. On the common people smiled and strolled on the paths and on the grass stepping round and over the dogshit while other people smiled and strolled as their dogs shitted on the paths and on the grass. The paddling pool was full of children. The sandbox, the roundabout, the swings, the rocking-horses and mums and dads were active on the playground. The washers of cars on our street were at it looking at the same time virtuous and given over to sensuality. The Greyhound Widow passed, her phantom husband dragging a silent foot. The trees had not so many leaves now, one day soon a heavy rain would leave them bare and winter would be here. 'Ah,' I said aloud standing at the window.

The Sunday papers were too many for me, they'd not get read today, I wasn't up to any intellectual activity. The turtles would be swimming, swimming and it occurred to me for the first time that for me they'd always be swimming. I'd never know whether they'd got to where they were going. At first I'd been obsessed with setting them free. Then it had become a heavy task I was committed to. Then we did it and afterwards it seemed a blank and empty thing. Now it felt a good thing again. The turtles were swimming to where they wanted to be. But that was *their* swimming, they couldn't do mine.

What was my swimming then? To go on working at the bookshop or somewhere else? To live alone or with someone? To stop smoking or not? To go on getting up in the morning or perhaps not? If I walked round the corner K257 would say 'I believe'. Believe what? I picked up the stone from Antibes. Look, Dad, here's a good one. Gone, gone, everything gone. Don't cry, Willy. I didn't. On the other hand, *do* cry, why not. I did.

I went downstairs. Miss Neap's *News of the World* was still lying in the hall by the front door, perhaps she'd decided to sleep in and let Sunday look after itself for once. I went over to the paddling pool. The children and the noise suddenly moved into close-up focus. A little boy punched a smaller one and seemed satisfied. Two little girls pranced splashing by, all flashing legs and flying hair. I dropped the stone from Antibes into the shallow water. It lay on the bottom looking up at me until the water glazed with light and I couldn't see the stone any more.

In the sunlight I went for a little walk down the New King's Road towards the Putney Bridge. They'd been resurfacing the road. Here and there were little huddles of air-compressors, asphalt-spreaders and rollers, red wooden tripods, yellow blinker lamps drawn up and bivouacked until Monday. At a zebra-crossing all the Belisha beacons were bagged in black plastic. I felt that one was never really alone while there was some-one to bag the Belisha beacons in black plastic.

I went back to my room. Evening was gathering in. The day hadn't been at all bad and this was the easy part, the downhill run. I didn't turn the lights on, let the room fill up with twilight and silence.

Mrs Inchcliff came back, unloaded her plunder and put it in the lumber-room, rattled about in the downstairs kitchen. I went out for fish and chips, brought it back to my room, ate by the light of the street lamps, had a beer.

There was a knock at the door. Mrs Inchcliff. 'Have you seen Miss Neap today?' she said.

'No,' I said, 'I haven't seen her since yesterday evening.'

'Neither have I,' she said. 'And I always do see her sometime on Sunday, either when she picks up her paper or when she goes out.'

'Perhaps she's gone to Leeds,' I said.

'I don't think so,' said Mrs Inchcliff. 'She was here last night when I went to bed, I saw her coming out of the bathroom. And if she'd left this morning she'd have taken the paper with her. I've just gone up to her room with it and knocked on the door but there was no answer. The door's on the latch but I didn't open it.'

We went down to Miss Neap's room on the first floor at the end of the hall. Mr Sandor coming in just then saw us and paused at the foot of the stairs. I opened the door, turned on the light.

Miss Neap had hanged herself. The window in her room was a tall one and at the top of it behind the pelmet there was a stout old iron hook screwed into the window-frame. It had been put there a long time ago for a curtain rod and drapes much heavier than the present ones. She'd stood on a chair and used several bright-coloured silk scarves knotted together. The chair lay on the floor where she'd kicked it over. She was dressed for the street in her tightly-belted leopard-skin coat and her newest purple suede boots. Her pince-nez had fallen off her nose and dangled from its ribbon. She must have been hanging there for some time, her face had gone quite dark and her powder and rouge and shiny blue eye-makeup looked ghastly. When the police doctor came he said the time of death had been between three and four on Sunday morning.

The room was in good order. She'd been there ten years, had done the place over and bought new furniture just as I'd done. The wallpaper and the drapes had a floral pattern. The bed was made up smartly into a green couch, colourful pillows carefully arranged on it and a large cloth Snoopy dog. Some paperback thrillers, some P. G. Wodehouse. A paperback *Four Quartets*. A copy of *The Book of Common Prayer* open at *At the Burial of the Dead at Sea*.

On the dresser were her Postal Savings book, a funeral directors' card and a receipt showing payment of £130. A note told us that arrangements had been made for cremation, that she wanted no funeral service of any kind whatsoever and that it was her wish that the cremation be completely unattended. Her mother in Leeds was not to be notified until after the cremation and her savings were then to be sent to her. The book showed a balance of £936.27. Next to it was a framed photograph of her mother and father and Miss Neap as a girl. No more than nine or ten years old but you could recognize the face as being the same one.

5

Neaera H.

I didn't know how lonely I'd been until the loneliness stopped. Now when I looked at my flat it seemed to have been cleared of invisible wires criss-crossed in patterns of pain that had been there for years. I saw myself in days past, years past, stepping carefully and trying to keep my balance. There were the kitchen, the bathroom, the sitting-room, the bedroom, the spare room. There were the books, the drawing-table, the typewriter, Madame Beetle, the clutter, all the spaces and places where I stood or sat or lay down, all the things that I touched and used in my daily effort to piece together an eggshell life from broken fragments.

George had given me so much that even if there came a time without George I could bear it now and not step carefully nor build my broken eggshell with mad patience. He hadn't done anything special, it was simply his way of being. Like him I found that I no longer minded being alive. And the turtles were swimming, there was always that to fall back on.

It was extraordinary, the whole turtle affair. Nothing was ever said about it in the press, there was no furore at the Zoological Society, George wasn't sacked. He let it be known that he'd set the large turtles free and would be replacing them with smaller specimens and that he would do the same again when the two remaining turtles were larger. That was all there was to it, he wasn't even reprimanded.

The two turtles in the tank looked different to me now, seemed less dozy and more as if they had something to look forward to:

> And every one said, 'If we only live,
> We too will go to sea in a Sieve, —
> To the hills of the Chankly Bore!'

I went to the British Museum again with my envelope full of blank paper. I felt friendly towards the coaches, cars and motorcycles in the forecourt, the people and the pigeons. I sat on the porch with the paper in my lap, sunlight again on my closed eyes.

I was waiting for something now and the waiting was pleasant. I was waiting for the self inside me to come forward to the boundaries from which it had long ago withdrawn. Life would be less quiet and more dangerous, life is risky on the borders. Gillian Vole and Delia Swallow live in safer places.

Come, I said to the self inside me. Come out and take your chance. After staring at the blank paper for a very long time I wrote:

> The fountain in the square
> Isn't there.

Well, I thought, it's not much but it's a beginning.

5 1

William G.

The Coroner's Court was a tall tight box with the lid always on it. Whatever was said in that room would not expand much laterally, would not move forward or back. It would stand and grow tall until its head touched the ceiling in the clear grey light.

The room seemed fully as tall as it was long. The dark green ceiling must have been at least twenty-five feet from the floor, deeply bevelled, with handsome white beams and braces. The walls were pale lemony green, there were tall windows, proper courtroom furniture: witness box, judge's bench, jury box. Just below the bench were red leather settees and a table with a red leather top for PRESS. Another such table for COUNSEL. A little plain narrow writing-stand for POLICE at the front of the spectators' pews. Ten Bibles in the jury box, two more by the witness box. There was a poor box by the door.

Three knocks. 'Rise, please, to Her Majesty's Coroner,' said the Coroner's Officer. We rose as the Coroner came in. 'Oyez, oyez, oyez,' said the Coroner's Officer as the Coroner passed to the bench, 'all manner of persons who have anything to do at this court before the Queen's Coroner touching upon the death of Flora Angelica Neap draw near and give your attendance. Pray be seated.'

We sat down. Behind the Coroner the royal arms

said *DIEU ET MON DROIT*. I counted the people in the room: the Coroner, the Coroner's Officer, the Police Pathologist and the constable who'd come to the house, a lady from the ticket agenwcy here Miss Neap had worked, a lady from the funeral directors, Mrs Inchcliff, Mr Sandor and me. Nine altogether. I wondered how long it had been since Miss Neap had had nine people pay attention to her all at once.

A frightening thought had been growing in me. I'd always assumed that I was the central character in my own story but now it occurred to me that I might in fact be only a minor character in someone else's. Miss Neap's perhaps. And I didn't even know the story. Draw near and give your attendance. Yes, we were doing that now. No one had done it when she was alive.

The constable testified that he had come to the house at a quarter to eight on Sunday evening and found the deceased lying on the couch where we'd put her. The pathologist testified that death had been from asphyxia due to hanging and had occurred between three and four that morning.

The lady from the ticket agency testified that Miss Neap had seemed in good spirits when she last saw her on Saturday and that she'd said she might go home at the weekend, she wasn't sure.

The lady from the funeral directors testified that Miss Neap had been last month to pay for her cremation, had said that she lived alone and it was something she wanted to take care of. Lived alone. I think Mrs Inchcliff, Mr Sandor and I all felt our faces go red at that.

Mrs Inchcliff, Mr Sandor and I swore in turn that we would speak the truth, the whole truth, and nothing but the truth but there was little more to be said than that Miss Neap had lodged at the house for ten years, that we had last seen her alive on Saturday evening looking much as usual and had found her dead on Sunday evening with the note, the Postal Savings book, the receipt and the funeral directors' card. Those were shown in evidence. The empty jury box seemed to fill up with blank-faced phantoms shaking their heads: Not the whole truth. But it was all we knew and all we could say. It stood there like a blind dumb thing and grew tall until its head touched the ceiling. The Coroner returned a verdict that Miss Neap had taken her own life and the court was adjourned.

The funeral directors were only a few minutes' walk down the street from the Coroner's Court. I wonder if Miss Neap had at some time taken the same walk. The lady who'd been at the inquest was a Mrs Mortimer. She was a handsome brownhaired woman who looked more like a theatrical wardrobe-mistress than a funeral director, she looked jolly and as if she ought to be in and out of actresses' dressing-rooms with pins in her mouth. Here was the place, a few urns and vases in the window. Inside was a plain little reception room.

'Everything's in order,' said Mrs Mortimer. 'She's having the "*Ely*", which is a standard cremation coffin with good class fittings. It'll be covered in purple dommett with a pink lining and she'll be wearing a pink robe. Plate of inscription on the lid with her name, age, date of death. It isn't right to send her off without a service, poor lady, and alone.'

'It's what she wanted,' I said. Sandor nodded emphatically.

'Do it how she wanted,' he said.

'That at least,' said Mrs Inchcliff.

'There's just one more thing,' said Mrs Mortimer. 'I hate to mention it but our prices went up last week. The *"Ely"* is now £121.50 instead of £109.50. The rest of it's the same: £7.00 for sanitizing and robing, £13.00 for the crematorium which includes the minister but I don't think I can get a rebate even if there's no service, 50p gratuity for the chappie at the crem. That comes to £142.00 instead of £130.00, so there's £12.00 owing.'

I wrote a cheque for the additional £12.00 for the '*Ely*'. So many things have names: wedding cakes, babies' prams, cars and coffins.

'Thank you,' said Mrs Mortimer. 'We'll have the body brought over from the mortuary. Cremation will be on Tuesday and she'll be here at the chapel of rest until then. In her instructions she said no viewing and no flowers please.'

No viewing, no flowers, no funeral service and no one at the cremation. Well, funerals are for the living. For good or ill one sees the dead removed from the scene and the departure is final. Miss Neap having been cheated of companionship while living wished to remain an undeparted presence when dead. Fair enough.

Miss Neap had died on Sunday, this was Thursday. That made four days running Sandor'd left the bath and cooker clean.

52

Neaera H.

It used to be that I stayed up till all hours and still felt time-starved, none of the day seemed to be metabolized into living. Now the minutes make me strong.

Frost this morning. Sharp it was, the air rang with it. I got up early and walked down the New King's Road to Parsons Green. Near where William lives there was a dead cat by a bus stop, pretty well flattened out. He looked as if he'd been run over by a lorry. A grey stripey tom he was with a head like a Roman senator, one eye open, one eye shut. His whole corpse seemed expressive of the WHAM! when his life met his death. He looked as if he'd been one hundred per cent alive until the lorry closed his account in the flower of his tomcathood and his mortal remains were cheerful rather than depressing. To live with a yowl and die with a WHAM! Thinking about him whilst walking back I stopped and wrote:

> Stiff but not formal
> A dead cat says hello
> This winter morning.

Later I'd be having lunch with George at the Aquarium: sandwiches by the salt-water tanks, the poshest spot in town. Between now and then were all kinds of minutes, all of them good. Who knew what might happen at the typewriter?

Before going up to the flat I went into the square, played hopscotch in it just as it was, with no fountain.

53

William G.

Autumn kept going with fewer and fewer brown and yellow leaves until a big rain came just as it always does. Wham! Bare trees, winter, black mornings, people walking fast.

This morning near the bus stop by a tree a dead cat said hello to me. There he was, he too had gone into winter with a wham. He looked as if he'd been flying high until he was brought down. I've never seen such a lively-looking dead cat.

The morning had nothing special to recommend it, the shop was full of people wanting biros and greeting cards, neither of which we sell. But I felt good.

At lunch-time I bought a bottle of Moët-Chandon and went up to the Zoo. In the tube I thought about Miss Neap and Mr Sandor and Mrs Inchcliff. With no funeral to go to we'd found ourselves drawn together somehow and remembering her but not altogether mournfully. In fact we all got drunk and Sandor sang gypsy songs. Rather well too. Odd but not really. If Flora Angelica Neap was going to be an undeparted presence she'd have to share the good times as well as the bad. And I could imagine good times, why I don't know. Nothing was different or better and I didn't think I was either but I didn't mind being alive at the moment. After all who knew what might happen?

Camden Town is the windiest tube station I know.

Coming up on the escalator with my hair flying I felt as if I was coming out of a dark place and into the light, then I laughed because that's what I was actually doing.

At the Aquarium I said hello to the two turtles, then opened various PRIVATE doors until I found George Fairbairn. Neaera was with him and they were eating sandwiches by the salt-water tanks. I gave George the champagne.

'I was just passing by,' I said, 'and I thought I'd drop this off.'

'Lovely,' said George. 'Cheers! What's the occasion?'

'Just that I was passing by,' I said.

They wanted me to stay and drink it with them but I couldn't stop. I took a taxi back to the shop, it was that kind of day.